DRUMS IN THE ABYSS
Rise of the Elder
Book I

By

Michael W. Garza

No part of this book may be reproduced or transmitted
in any form or by any electronic or mechanical means, including
photocopying, recording, or by any information and retrieval
system, without the written permission of the author, except
where permitted by law.

This is a work of fiction. Names, characters, places, and
incidents are the product of the author's imagination or
are used fictitiously. Any resemblance to actual events,
locales, or persons, living or dead, is purely coincidental.

ISBN: 978-0-9979004-9-1

Proofread by Karen Robinson of
INDIE Books Gone Wild.

The oldest and strongest emotion of mankind is fear.

And the oldest and strongest kind of fear is fear of the unknown.

-H.P. Lovecraft

ALSO BY MICHAEL W. GARZA

The Decaying World Saga

The Hand That Feeds

The Last Infection

Tribes of Decay

Season of Decay

Cult of the Elder Mythos

The Elder Unearthed

(A collection of tales)

Vision of the Elder

NeverHaven

Children of the Mark

Rise of the Elder

Drums in the Abyss

The Shadow Gate Chronicles

The Last Shadow Gate

A Veil of Shadows

1

Professor William Markinson wrote June 19 in the top right corner of his journal and then slammed it closed in frustration. His archeological team had been lost down in the abominable caves west of the city of Bursa for nearly a full day. Their faithful guide Ahmed continued his pursuit of their freedom from the darkness. The professor feared none of them had faith that a joyful ending awaited.

There were five in the group, including Professor Markinson's assistant Alex Reed; the jack-of-all-trades, Ms. Lauren Miller; Ahmed; and his nephew, Emre. It was by the professor's insistence that they were there, and he was miserable for it. His passion for uncovering the truth behind the Cult of the Elder overwhelmed him far beyond his common sense, and he feared the worst was yet to come.

"I need a moment," the professor said, holding up his hand. "Just some time to catch my breath."

There was a collective groan from the group but no real detractors. Each of them sat down on the cold stone ground in a loose circle. Lauren furiously typed away on her tablet. Alex joined the professor before too long.

"We seem to be descending," Alex said, whispering. He was critical of Ahmed and had expressed his reservations numerous times about continuing to follow the guide. "I'm sure we should have given an effort to climb the fracture in the rock we found an hour ago." It was the third time he reminded the professor of his suggestion since Ahmed disagreed with him. "We should go it alone," he mumbled to himself.

Professor Markinson had grown tired of Alex's constant complaining, but he reminded himself that Alex was only there by his request. As a graduate student, under his personal guidance for an entire year, Alex was the logical choice to join the expedition.

However, their relationship at the university had not prepared the professor for dealing with the young man's personality quirks in such a stressful situation.

"What would you have me do?" Professor Markinson snapped back louder than he had intended. "Do you want to wander off in the dark? Would we really have been any better off if we'd taken another path?"

Alex recoiled from the verbal lashing as his eyes widened in the dim light. The glow of the assorted flashlights flickered, and the shadows danced across his frightened face. He regained his composure and then slid his narrow glasses up the bridge of his nose with his index finger. The loud reply caused a stir in Ahmed, but he pretended not to notice the verbal confrontation.

"I just...we could...."

Professor Markinson waved off Alex's attempt at an explanation.

"I apologize," he said. "I'm afraid the long trek has gotten the best of me." The professor took a long, slow breath and then lowered his voice. "Let's give him a bit more time." His eyes slid toward Ahmed. "He knows what he's doing."

Alex nodded but did not respond; instead, he looked down at the pale glow of his phone. Professor Markinson did not wait for anything more. No one had gotten a signal on their phones since the moment they lowered themselves down into the initial chamber to the caves. The unbearable Turkish heat vanished with the last view of the surface. The constant chill in the air made them all regret their complaints about the heat on their jeep ride out from the city.

Professor Markinson glanced from Alex to Lauren and then to Ahmed. In truth, the group had little choice but to continue to follow their guide. Professor Markinson believed him to be hopelessly lost, although Ahmed's pride would not allow him to admit it. They had enough rations to last five days, and the professor feared that as the supplies dwindled, so would their morale. Lauren's flashlight came to life, and she directed the beam along one side of the cave. She ran her finger over the stone and then rubbed it against her thumb. If her deductions offered any hope, she was not willing to share.

"Let us continue," Ahmed said as he got to his feet and stretched. The dark-skinned man nearly disappeared as he stepped away from his nephew's lantern. "We must keep moving."

Alex sighed deeply as he stood but otherwise kept his comments to himself. It was more than the collective desire to see the light of day again that urged them to keep moving, and Professor Markinson knew it. There was a fear in the air that he could not explain, which mimicked the growing beat in his heart. He had heard sounds in the darkness. The others did not speak of it, and he was beginning to question his sanity. A faint wavering thud beat somewhere beyond them. At times, it imitated the professor's heart, at other times, his every step.

"Pick up the pace," Ahmed said from the front in his heavily accented voice.

Ahmed led as if their destination were within reach. The professor could not fault him; his courage was far more than he could ever muster. Ahmed's tall, wide-shouldered frame exuded confidence. He carried the hard chin of a man whom other men would follow into battle. Among the group, it was Emre, which the professor felt sorry for the most. The boy could not be more than thirteen, and the dread in his eyes was blatant. He had not spoken aloud in several hours.

Their present direction led in a lowering angle with little more to guide them than long cracks in the stone and murkiness ahead of the lamp light. The professor was unsure what bewilderment had overcome the group to hold back the terror that should have swept their courage away, but he was grateful for it. Dreary shadows stretched across the cold, stone walls, shifting with every step. Exhaustion played havoc with the professor's imagination. He could not stave off the inevitable panic that was sure to consume him.

A sudden shout from the front of the loose formation pulled him from his spiraling deliberation.

"Professor, look at this."

Ahmed was down on one knee, clutching something in his hand; Lauren was next to him with Emre holding the lamp above the gathering.

"Now that seems out of place," Lauren said before Professor Markinson could figure out what they were looking at. "Don't you think?" She slipped her long bangs behind her ears and moved out of the way.

Professor Markinson took a long look at what Ahmed was holding, but he could not bring himself to identify it for a second. He leaned in closer to the find, and there was no denying that the carved piece of stone was the head of an ax. Ahmed gave it to him, and everyone's eyes locked on the professor as if he might surmise something far beyond their capabilities. He turned the stone and ran his fingers over its side. The smoothness indicated a great deal of skill in its making. Alex's voice echoed around the group.

"What do you think, Professor?"

"A fairly common discovery," he said. "Only it's about six thousand miles from where I would expect to find it."

"I do not follow," Ahmed said.

Excluding his nephew, Ahmed was the least historically educated of the group.

"You see the curvature along the top of the ax head?" the professor asked as he ran his finger across its length. "This is something you might find in an excavation in the central states of North America, possibly even as far south as Mexico, but here...." He considered the possibilities but found himself at a loss.

Alex took the opportunity to interject. He had a way of highlighting his knowledge without obviously boasting. This talent wore on the professor, and the expressions from the others said he was not alone.

"There are other examples of fossils discovered in unlikely locations," Alex announced. "The Anders-Myer expedition of Antarctica in 1919, for example," Alex spouted the encyclopedia reference with considerable skill. He was a fountain of rare knowledge. "They found arrowheads and even the remains of a headdress piece some half a mile beneath the ice surface. To my knowledge, no one has ever been able to account for it."

The professor removed a handkerchief from his pocket and wrapped the ax head in it. "Then let us pray that we shall have an opportunity to inquire about the history of our find."

They began to walk again. The ax head provided them with the distraction they needed for a time. As far as the professor could gather, there was no logical reasoning to find a weapon of that design so far from its natural location. He pondered the issue for as long as it would occupy his mind, trying to ignore the guilt tearing at his gut.

The promise of finding the truth behind the Cult of the Elder brought them to Bursa and the endless valley to the west of the city. The fissure that led them down into the caves beneath the earth hinted at answers to questions the professor had searched for over four decades. It appeared to him now that the Elder's secrets might remain beyond his reach. He ran his hand through the close-cropped hairs of his salt and pepper beard. He imagined each strand could count for every dead end in his endless search. The surrounding darkness said his pursuit would most likely come to a less than glorious culmination.

An hour passed before Ahmed called them to a halt. The professor was hopeful they would find another artifact that may in some way correlate with, or at least provide some additional insight on, the true nature of their first find. However, he was unprepared for what the light from Emre's lamp revealed. Complete awe consumed him. The dreaded tunnel had come to an abrupt end. A new way opened into the dark in opposing directions, but it was the stone directly in front of them or, more precisely, the carving in the rock, which astounded them.

The professor gently ran his hand over the hieroglyphics as if they might crumble at the touch. He could hear the awe spew from Alex as he looked over his shoulder. The professor had only recently shared with his assistant some of the factual findings of his labor to uncover the truth behind the Cult of the Elder. The professor knew Alex recognized the symbols on the wall from the book of the Fallen Star, which was the pride of the professor's collection on the subject matter.

"Is that Egyptian?" Lauren asked.

"No," Professor Markinson said.

Lauren had not been his first choice for the expedition. She came highly recommended, but she had very little insight as to his true aims.

"This is a foul thing," Ahmed said in a low tone to his nephew. He did not possess formal schooling; however, his knowledge of the legends of his people ran deep. The locals had hefty respect for their former tribal beliefs, and the faith in the Elder gods was a long-standing tradition.

The professor had little doubt that Ahmed knew what the writing meant.

"You are pleased?" Ahmed asked.

The professor did not answer right away. He removed his pack with Alex's assistance and found the thick, ancient book he sought. He removed some papers from the cover on which he had worked a premise of sorts for translation. He mulled over the carvings on the wall with heated anticipation as Alex copied down his every word. The process was slow going, but they managed with a great deal of success.

"From the heavens, the stars fall," Alex read aloud from what he had written down. "The ageless ones bring life. Walk the great city of Morgainok and offer your soul."

Everyone stood in haunting silence, waiting for the words to have some meaning they could grasp. The professor knew all too well what they found and could barely contain his excitement.

"Professor, it's as you hoped it would be," Alex said. "Morgainok."

"You knew there was a city buried here?" Ahmed asked.

"Hoped," he said.

"We are trapped," Lauren countered. "Doomed to die no doubt, and you say you hoped for this?"

She wore her anger plain on her face. Her eyes narrowed as she attempted to stare scornfully at the professor and Alex at the same time. The lines of her face hinted at her age, but she managed to hold onto the good looks of her youth.

"Of course not," Professor Markinson said. "I will not deny that the search for Morgainok was my true purpose, but I never intended to lose myself in the process. Do not be absurd," he added for good measure.

It was clear to see the argument that was to come. Professor Markinson was in no mood for such a thing, but a faint sound ended the coming storm. The look in Lauren's eyes told the professor she heard it too. Distant but distinct, the thudding rose in a rhythmic pulse. Alex's eyes bulged as he tried to peer through the darkness. The group held still as if somehow their motionless stance would make the noise go away. There was no denying it now, the beating sound was calling, and Professor Markinson knew for sure that it was summoning them all.

2

The sound was authentic. Lauren had heard the distant beating several times during the group's aimless walk, but she was never confident it was anything more than her imagination playing tricks on her. Her anger had kept her from being afraid, but the anger was fading. She had seen the look on the others' faces, and their panic was contagious.

The fear that followed did not come all at once. Like pinpricks, Lauren felt the onslaught of fright take hold. This fear was communal. Ahmed drew his pistol, believed to be the only such weapon among the group. Emre dimmed his lamp, and they stood like statues until their knees ached.

"What devil of a thing lurks here?" Ahmed asked.

Lauren's eyes followed the guide's stare toward the professor. The older man was quiet, holding his hand up to make his point. Lauren instinctively slid her hand around to the small of her back until her fingertips grazed the hard exterior grip of her 9mm. Professor Markinson was against the use of weapons and only gave into Ahmed's demand to bring one after he refused to guide them without it.

"Superstitious nonsense," the professor said. "My study of the occult is fueled by academic curiosity of what these people believed or what some of them still believe, but not what I believe myself. This represents a monumental archeological find and proves the Cult of the Elder has its roots buried in some four thousand years of history." His passion for the subject appeared to overtake him.

"And whatever makes that noise is something you do not believe in either?" Ahmed asked.

The question left the professor's response caught somewhere in his throat. Lauren knew of the Cult of the Elder but only in passing. She had little interest in the subject and grew irritated with herself for not checking further into the professor before accepting his invitation. The truth was that she needed the money. An annoying voice in the back of her head said she would have signed on even if he had been upfront about his true expectations. She pulled her hand away from her gun and decided it was best to keep the secret to herself.

"Is there anything else you would like to tell us?" Lauren asked, glancing from Alex to Professor Markinson. She felt like saying *tell me,* but for the time being, she figured Ahmed and Emre had been as left in the dark as her.

"I have told you precisely what you need to know," the professor said. "And paid you half upfront for your effort, if you will remember."

Lauren was not sure the amount paid was sufficient to cover their current predicament, but she was not in any position to make changes to their arrangement. She decided instead of arguing that she would put her considerable skills to use. Lauren was involved in numerous expeditions in the valley of Sangarius and spoke several of the local dialects. She had an itching feeling that the professor had other plans for who should have made up his team but had simply run out of alternates. The professor's patience was waning.

"You do remember getting paid, don't you?"

Lauren did not answer, nor did she see the point in quarreling. Neither their discovery of the hieroglyphics nor the acknowledgment of the distant sounds made any changes to their dire circumstances. She motioned Ahmed to continue and then stepped past the professor and Alex to join the guide out front, heading down the tunnel in the direction of the sound.

The noise grew steadily with every passing step. A faint glow glimmered in the darkness far ahead. Lauren saw to the extinguishing of the lamps and flashlights, and the distant glow gave away the outline of an opening in the tunnel. The cavity doubled in size as they neared the end.

"What in the world," Lauren said when her eyes adjusted to the darkness. She slipped out her phone from her pocket and hit record as she got down on a knee. "That's something you don't see every day."

The cavern walls were inlaid with a substance she could not rightly identify. The faint glow in the rock was the result of the substance embedded in the stone. The lines of light ran far up into the rock face above them. It gave the appearance of an open sky and an endless sea of stars. Lauren stared at the rock as if overcome with madness.

"It's flowing like water," Alex said before she could get it out. "How is that even possible?"

She was glad that she was not the only one at a loss for explanations. Lauren chipped at the rock with a small tool and exposed the liquid beneath. The pale light faded to darkness the instant the substance was exposed to the air.

"This would be much more interesting if I thought we could actually share it with someone," she said, muttering to herself.

Emre moved around her, the faint light silhouetting the boy as he continued forward. He stopped several paces ahead of Lauren, where the tunnel turned. His sudden, frantic wave caused everyone to rush forward at once. Lauren reached him first, and his discovery stretched her bewilderment beyond any time before. The tunnel opened up to a cavern a size unimaginable in her mind. The immensity of it swallowed her whole and provided a profound sense of insignificance.

"Professor?"

Lauren's eyes slid from the vast dark space out above them and down into a massive bowl beneath them. The view stole her breath. Rising from the cavern floor was the outline of endless towers and bizarrely shaped structures, each highlighted by the pale threads of light. A number of the structures climbed several stories high. In the distance, standing high above the dark city was the most impressive sight of all. An enormous pyramid dominated the cityscape like no other. Constructed in the squared style of Chichen Itza, a long staircase lay centered on one side.

Professor Markinson's whispered response frightened Lauren. "Morgainok."

"This is unholy ground," Ahmed said. "The forgotten death."

"Gibberish," Alex countered. "You do not understand the importance of this find." He pointed out at the sprawling city. "An advanced people who no doubt were the foundation of the myths and legends of your people." His voice carried far off the surrounding rock. "Professor Markinson has long believed that the superstitions of your ancestors are little more than fantastic explanations for the unknown, an unknown that could only come from a far advanced people—"

"Alex."

Lauren was grateful the professor cut off his star pupil. His condescending tone was getting on her nerves. Her experience with locals told her Ahmed was far from an ignorant farmer. She also guessed from the size of his arms that he could pound Alex to a pulp if he pushed the man beyond his limits. She had a quick desire to see Alex put in his place, although the confrontation would not help her get out of the current predicament.

"What do you suggest we do?" she asked Ahmed.

He kept his mouth closed for a time, sweeping his stare over their enormous discovery.

"It would seem reasonable to me," he said after giving the question considerable thought, "that a city so grand would not have been intended to survive below ground alone."

Lauren followed his reasoning.

"While we have stumbled upon an entrance," Ahmed said, continuing. "There must surely have been other such passages in and out."

Lauren shifted her stance with noticeable hesitation. "You mean to take us down there?" she asked.

Ahmed looked to the professor and then back to her. "I do," he said.

"Do not concern yourself," the professor said before she could object. "The trappings of such a place would have been long destroyed. Judging by the sheer size of it, I would say our deepest concern should be avoiding aimless wandering."

His explanation did not put her mind at ease. She would have been happy to turn around and attempt to find another way out of the catacombs behind them. Lauren wanted someone to at least attempt to explain the thumping beat they all heard while studying the hieroglyphics. More so, she was pretty confident the professor and perhaps Alex was keeping details about the cult to themselves.

She silently ran through the few particulars she knew about the Cult of the Elder. There was an extensive black market for cult-related artifacts, one, reputable universities and collectors would not acknowledge doing business with, although most did. She did not count Professor Markinson among the kind who were on the hunt for personal gain, which left him in one of two categories. Either he was someone who actually believed the cult, and its gods were a living, breathing thing, or he was a part of one of the modern-day factions searching for his own personal archaeological holy land. Both choices painted him as at least half crazy by Lauren's standards.

She slipped her backpack off and set it on the ground. Lauren rummaged through the meager gear and cursed at Alex under her breath. The faithful assistant had lost the main supply bag on their initial descent into the caves. She was unsure what she was looking for; there was no signal down in the caves, and a quick check of her phone confirmed their entrance into the underground city would be no different. Lauren got back to her feet and settled her sights on Ahmed.

"After you."

◆

The way down into Morgainok was less of a hike and more of a steep climbing descent. Lauren held on with both hands, struggling to find a space wide enough to put her feet. She felt the burn rising up her back and into her shoulders. A yelp escaped her mouth a split second before the tip of her boot dug in. The pain in her arms subsided as she had to take a moment to breathe and convince herself that she was not about to tumble to her death.

"Ms. Miller."

It took Lauren a second to realize someone was talking to her. As far as she could remember, Ms. Miller was her mother. She was not used to formal acknowledgment, but she had been called much worse. Emre's heavy accent gave him away as the caller before she turned her face to get a look at him.

"Are you okay?"

His sorrowful expression told her that her attempt to show the men she would not struggle with the climb had failed.

"I will survive," she said, not definite that it was true. "How are you holding up?"

The boy's mouth parted in a gentle smile. "I can climb anything," he said, then hung away from the rock face with one hand to make his point.

Lauren's heart fluttered. "All right, all right, I get it," she said, motioning for him to grab a hold. "No need to show off."

He smiled again and then continued climbing down. Lauren took one last breath and then slid a hand further down, followed by the other hand. A glance said they were midway between the lip of the tunnel above and the massive cavern floor. Ahmed had led them down, and he appeared to be close to the bottom.

Lauren focused on the task, but her mind pondered on what

awaited them. The thumping sounds had not returned, and she was grateful for it. She was not sure her mind could deal with anything else going wrong. She kept telling herself that they would soon stumble across a way out, but her common sense was beginning to get in the way of that idea. Lauren had been on countless expeditions from the frozen outlands of Russia to the darkest points of Africa. Each adventure had its own set of challenges, but she had managed to make it through every turn.

She contemplated the likelihood of her survival until the whispered sounds of the men conversing reached her ears. She was a few feet from the cavern floor when she let go of the wall, and the fall resulted in a solid thud. Emre was close to her, obviously trying to hear what the men were saying without looking like he was paying attention. She patted the boy on the shoulder as she moved toward the quorum.

The dark city rose around them with jagged, crumbling fortifications. Lauren's eyes adjusted to the light within the walls, and many stone walkways appeared between the structures. The eerie glow was powerful enough to forgo the lanterns and flashlights, but Lauren lit her light anyway, if for no other reason than to keep some control over her surroundings. Her eyes were drawn to the odd structures a few arm lengths away as she came to a stop.

"Well, let's not have any more secrets," she said as she approached the men. "I think we've got plenty of those to keep us busy for a while."

The remark drew the ire of Professor Markinson and a noticeable snarl from Alex. Ahmed's flared nostrils were easy to read.

"They want to walk straight into the heart of the devil," he exclaimed.

Lauren was still trying to process his anger when Alex elaborated enough for her to fill in the blanks.

"This is an ancient city," Alex said, "filled with the artifacts of a civilization that is virtually unknown to the modern world.

We cannot possibly ignore the historical value of what we have found."

"You want to go toward that pyramid structure," Lauren said, deducing the argument. "I think we should take a—"

"No," Ahmed cut in. "I will not step foot on that unholy ground. I will lead us around this godforsaken place and find another way out."

The professor put his hands up as he stepped into the center of the group. "Ahmed," he said in a calm voice, "We respect your beliefs."

Lauren doubted that very much, but she kept her comments to herself.

"I can assure you," Professor Markinson continued. "We will not desecrate this place or do anything to bring some form of hex against you or your family."

Ahmed's shoulders relaxed, but he kept his hands on his hips in a defiant stance.

"Perhaps we can find a middle ground," Alex offered.

Ahmed looked at Lauren, and she realized he wanted her opinion on the matter.

"We're already here," she heard herself say. "We could explore some of the ruins as we look for a way out." The truth was that she was on both sides of the argument. The professor paid Lauren upfront for her involvement with the expedition, but she would also receive a percentage of any money made based on the find. "No pyramid."

Her final notion drew harsh scowls from Alex and the professor, but she did not care. Lauren figured she wanted to keep herself in Ahmed's good graces as long as she could. If their situation grew any worse than it already was, his abilities would be far more helpful than the university pair. Alex took the opening to disagree.

"I didn't say that," he argued. "There are no ghosts here. There is no such thing as evil spirits." The condescension in his tone was difficult to ignore. "There's too much at stake to walk away from." He threw his hands out wide as he turned toward the dark city now only a few feet away. "For God's sakes, look at what we found."

Ahmed shook his head. "You do not know everything."

Alex chuckled. "There's nothing to be afraid of," he said. The professor tried to cut him off, but Alex continued. "There is no one here—"

Lauren thought perhaps the argument had ended, but a scan of the men's faces said otherwise. They were quiet, silent as a grave. She began to speak when Ahmed held his hand up to stop her. Lauren nearly screamed when Emre brushed past her and drew in close to his uncle.

The cause of the sudden stir revealed itself in a rising sound. The thumping washed over the fortifications and slipped through the dark walkways toward the new arrivals. The sound was more apparent than ever before and unmistakable. The rhythmic beating of drums was in melodic tune.

Ahmed's voice cut through the shock of the moment with his own dose of condescension. "You were saying?"

3

The drumming stopped, and the silent void left behind was enough to suck the air out of the entire cavernous city. Professor Markinson had to remind himself to breathe. He tried to rationalize what he had heard, searching frantically for any reasonable explanation. He looked back at the eyes of his awaiting group and stammered.

"There's probably...caves that...echo...."

He stopped when Ahmed threw up his hands and turned away, pulling his nephew with him. "I have heard enough," Ahmed said.

"Wait a minute," the professor declared and then glanced at Alex for some assistance.

"The climb is too difficult," Alex said.

Ahmed stood looking up at the sheer rock face they had climbed down. He had his hands on his hips. He stood silent for a long time before shaking his head and turning back to the group.

"This is no game," Ahmed said, his accent deeper than ever before. "You have searched for the devil itself, and you have found it."

Professor Markinson looked at Lauren and gauged her support of their guide.

"We do not know what we have found," the professor admitted. He still could not convince himself that what they heard was coming from somewhere in the city. There was no logical sense to the idea, and it simply would not fit. He swept the idea away all at once and felt a resurgence to his confidence. "This is a once-in-a-lifetime opportunity," he said with renewed self-assurance. "And I will not allow you to take that away from this team."

Lauren's face twitched at the sound of the declaration, but he chose to ignore it.

"You were hired to do a job," the professor continued. "Will you continue to do it or not?"

Ahmed's eyes narrowed as he glared at the professor. He put a hand on Emre's shoulder and worked his stare from the professor to Alex then back again.

"I will agree to search for another way out of this place," he said with much disdain. "And it seems I can only do this by continuing forward."

Professor Markinson did not consider Ahmed's statement an agreement, but he would take it under the circumstances. Ahmed drew his gun and pushed Emre ahead. The boy tugged on Lauren's wrist before turning up his lamp and lifting it to light the way. Professor Markinson let the trio pass and then fell in line behind them with Alex at his side.

Morgainok was a remarkable sight. The evenly laid black-stone walkways ran between rows of edifices reaching up high above. Their initial view confirmed that the walls of the surrounding structures were not carved from the cavern itself. The black rock must have been brought in from somewhere else and carefully set in place. The idea of the task was fascinating. Professor Markinson knew the feat would have been monstrous by current standards, but how it was accomplished or even planned was unimaginable thousands of years ago.

The buildings did not appear to have roofs of any kind. Most were simple structures consisting of little more than four walls. An initial scan did not produce any signs of doorways or entrances. The professor got a glimpse of spiral towers in the distance, several stories tall, and he could not imagine the purpose. Platforms opened up high on the higher bastions, and odd stone spikes adorned the uppermost points.

"Professor."

Alex's call drew the professor out of his fascinated inspection. He shook at the first word above a whisper since they entered the city. His gut churned as he tried to calm his nerves. Alex and Lauren were up ahead of him, standing by an opening in the face of the rock. Ahmed was down on one knee, pistol at the ready. The hair on the professor's neck rose at the sight of the man's apparent fear. Emre waved at Professor Markinson as the boy whispered.

"They found something."

The professor closed the distance in a few long strides, his heartbeat rising with every step. He pulled in close behind the others and peered through the opening. The structure's interior was narrow and bare save for an opening in the ground, which dominated the space. The faint light in the walls reflected off clear water within the hole. There was little else to see.

Lauren took a hesitant step forward and then knelt at the edge of the opening on the floor. She shined her flashlight on the water as if expecting to see something lurking down beneath. The professor followed her in, drawn to the hole, enticed by its purpose. Lauren slid the beam across the surface then up at the gap beneath the edge of the floor.

"It's hollow underneath," she said.

The professor moved closer at her assertion and found she was correct. The discovery stirred his fear, but for the life of him, he could not explain why. He could not piece together the use of the place or the idea of what type of people once lived there. An abrupt noise caused him to leap back. Lauren spun around, pulling a pistol from her belt. She cut him off before he could get the words out.

"Do not even bother," she said, moving past him and out into the walkway. "You're just as glad to see another gun as I am that I brought it."

It took a moment for the professor to realize Alex was missing. Ahmed and Emre were farther ahead, both looking at another structure. Professor Markinson kept up with Lauren until the entire group was together again. He heard Alex's voice before he saw him.

"That was close."

Alex stepped out into the open, sloshing water on the ground as he went. He leaned over and gulped in the air. The professor looked him over and discovered the young assistant was drenched from the waist down. It took a moment to sink in, but everyone figured it out before Alex gave himself away.

"I took a bad step," Alex said.

Lauren laughed aloud but then managed to choke the rest of it down when Alex scowled at her.

"Next time, you might not come back up," the professor snapped. "What did you find?"

Alex shook off the cold remark and waddled as he turned. He shined the light on the interior base of a tower and revealed a much bigger space than the first one they found. The pool Alex graciously located was set in the center of the floor, but there were several new additions to the floorplan.

Professor Markinson studied what appeared to be a series of tables built into the wall opposite the entryway, each with an assortment of unique oddities strewn across the top. He shifted to the first of an ascending row of spikes jutting out from the wall and followed them up the center of the hollowed-out interior to the very peak of the structure. The crude staircase had considerable gaps between each step, and he could not speculate its usefulness to a man his size. A few hesitant paces took him beyond the pool of water, and he could not rationalize the sudden fear creeping over him.

"Professor."

Lauren's beckon brought him to a stop. He attempted to shake off the growing haze, clouding his intellect.

"Calm yourself," he said and waved her in. "I want to examine this."

He stopped at the foot of the nearest table and allowed the light to fill the far wall as Lauren and Alex approached. The table was carved directly out of the surrounding rock, hinting at skill and precision. Across the top lay a half dozen objects, each as black as the wall. Professor Markinson picked one up and held it up in the light.

He assumed it was an idol of sorts, making out two pairs of arms, joined at a slender torso. The thing's head was a foul creation, with an open mouth covering most of its face. Several tentacles protruded from the orifice, positioned up above its head. The professor had a sudden desire to toss the vile sculpture back down where he found it, but Alex reached out for it before he had the chance to act.

"Amazing," Alex said as he took it.

"Indeed," the professor said and then glanced at the entrance. Ahmed and Emre stood beyond the opening, neither willing to take a step inside. "Just give us a moment."

Ahmed nodded and then turned his attention back to the walkway.

"That might actually be useful," Lauren said and motioned for the stairs. "We could get a look around and at least get a sense of direction."

She was at the base of the steps by the time the professor looked up.

"I am not sure," he said, shaking his head. "It's more likely that we'll kill ourselves trying to climb to the top."

Lauren's eyes ran the length of the distance between each of the jutting spikes. The professor guessed her calculations before she announced them.

"Why are they so far apart?"

The question hung in the air for a minute, and the silence caused Alex to break away from his study of the idol.

"Perhaps they are not stairs at all," the professor said.

Neither Lauren nor Alex offered up a counterargument. Lauren shrugged off her reservations and climbed up on the first spike. Her wobbling balance convinced Professor Markinson to join her. He stood off the side, ready to grab her if need be while she readied herself to jump up to the next spike. The professor saw the uselessness of the exercise almost immediately.

"And how exactly do you plan to get back down?" he asked. "Assuming you do not break your neck on the climb."

Lauren ignored him for a time and then sprang forward and hit the center of the next spike with a perfect landing.

"It's called rope," she said without looking back at him. "This isn't my first rodeo, you know."

The off-hand comment was enough to get the professor to back away. He and Alex looked on as Lauren continued her climb. The woman had considerably more athletic ability than they had imagined. She was near the highest point of the structure before she spoke again.

"There's access to the ceiling," she called down. "Just one more."

Professor Markinson saw the jump that followed the announcement, and he knew at once that something was wrong. Lauren's muffled cry preceded the tumbling beam of light. Her flashlight hit the stone ground a second later with a loud crash and promptly went black. The professor already had one leg up on the bottom spike when Alex cast his light on Lauren's dangling feet.

"Hold on," Professor Markinson yelled as he steadied himself in preparation for the jump ahead. "Keep the light on her."

He managed to get himself up but had to keep his hand on the wall to stay balanced. The professor was estimating the next jump when something caught his attention. His eyes were on Lauren's legs as she swept them over the highest spike in the structure, but he could not will himself to move. She managed to lie prone, wrapping both hands around the extension, and then froze as everyone focused squarely on the renewed beating of the drums. Professor Markinson's heart froze up in his chest as something clenched his leg.

"That's close."

Alex's murmured utterance was enough to infuriate him.

"Let go of me, you damn fool."

Lauren righted herself in silence and then slowly slid her head up through the opening in the structure. Professor Markinson and Alex looked on, listening to the drums' rising sound, neither attempting to climb higher. Lauren's scan was short-lived. She tied off the rope and then tossed the end down. Her frantic repel caused a stir in the professor that he could not explain. He held the rope in place as she finished her climb. Lauren stood between the professor and Alex in the muted glow, trying desperately to stop herself from shaking. Professor Markinson held his tongue until he could not stand it any longer.

"What did you see?"

She looked up at him, eyes wide and lost, as if only then realizing she was not alone. Her response was quick and jumbled. "They're moving. They're coming."

The professor waited for details that she obviously was not going to provide. "Who?" he asked and then corrected himself. "What is coming?"

She tried to collect her thoughts. "I could see all around us," she explained, "in every direction. The glow in the rock lit up countless walkways and buildings, all leading toward that pyramid at the center of the city." She stopped, and her eyes narrowed. "There were outlines, moving with the beat of the drums."

"Outlines of what?" Alex asked as he edged closer.

"People," she said slowly. "Or something else."

A question slipped out before Professor Markinson could stop himself. "What, else?"

Lauren shook her head. "It was just outlines, really," she said. "But they were unnaturally tall, swaying more than striding." She snapped back to the present. "I could not make out anything else."

The professor decided not to press her on the details. The logical part of him said she was seeing things, and the glow within the rock was playing tricks on her mind. He did not want to acknowledge another part of him, even to himself, which said they were not alone in Morgainok. He found himself locked in place, and he could feel the eyes of his group focused squarely on him, waiting for him to give them direction.

"We should...uh." He looked around at them, pausing on Emre outside the entrance to the structure. "We should continue through the city and look for another opening—"

"Did you not hear me?" Lauren said, cutting in. "There's something out there, someone out there." Professor Markinson shook his head, but she did not let him continue. "Listen to that sound." She paused to allow the rhythmic thumping to overtake her words. "They're coming, and I think they know we're here."

Alex backed away from the argument. He glanced at the professor but refused to hold the stare. Professor Markinson took a step toward the opening and turned his back on Lauren.

"There's no one down here," he said more for himself than anyone else. "The people of the dark city have been extinct for centuries."

"Keep telling yourself that," Lauren said behind him. "I just want to get the hell out of here."

The professor continued out into the walkway and waited until the entire group was gathered.

"Let's continue," he said to Ahmed.

The dark man's face was easy to read. He no longer wanted any part of the city or the professor's expedition. He was close to his nephew, with one hand around the back of the boy's neck and his other hand firmly gripped around his gun. He did not speak, instead nodding his acceptance of the order.

Ahmed did not manage a step before the beating of the drums came to a stop. He froze mid-step as the haunting quiet overtook the group. They held still for an agonizingly long time. The professor waited until he could no longer stand it, but before he urged the others to move, the unmistakable sound of footsteps echoed around him from somewhere in the dark.

4

The footsteps were, in truth, very close. Lauren stood motionless; sure something was about to jump out and grab her at any second. She did not know what she saw from the top of the structure, and she did not care whether the professor believed her or not. Her nerves were shot, and what was worse, she had lost her damn flashlight.

The gun shook in her hand, and she could not remember pulling it out. Lauren relied on Alex's light. She followed the beam with the barrel of her gun as the light feverishly whipped back and forth across the walkway. There was no doubt in her mind that the footsteps were drawing closer.

"We cannot stay here," Ahmed whispered. "We are out in the open. We need to keep moving."

Lauren agreed, but she could not convince herself to say it aloud. She was terrified and mad all at the same time. The terror was clearly from the situation, but the anger came from her response to the situation. She had been in enough hairy conditions to prove she could take care of herself. She felt she needed to remember that to stop her heart from beating out of her chest, if for nothing else.

Ahmed started forward, and the group followed, staying in a close huddle directly behind him. The anxiety was palpable, surrounding them with a choking force. Lauren could sense it in every muscle of her body and every hair on her head. She had to prompt herself to move for the first several strides.

The footsteps had stopped sometime between when the group first heard them and Ahmed's encouragement to continue. Lauren did not like the idea of not knowing who or what was coming. The dim structures grew in height the further the group ventured into the city. They bypassed several entrances without so much as a word. It was not until they stepped out into a wide-open space that Ahmed finally halted.

The glow of the pale light in the rock outlined a tall barrier running around the length of a roughly squared area. The now-familiar structures lined the exterior of the space, none of them erected within the boundary. The beam of Alex's flashlight traversed one side of the open zone to the other, revealing several peculiarities. The glimmer of water dotted the floor from sporadically placed holes, none of them similar in size or shape. The light came to a final rest on a tall figure, which nearly caused Lauren to fire off a round at first glance.

"It's like the piece we found," Alex said, holding up the small, carved idol the professor discovered. "Amazing."

Amazing was not the descriptor Lauren would have chosen. She forced herself to holster her gun in the small of her back, deciding she was more likely to kill one of her team members under the circumstances. She stepped past Alex and urged Emre to follow her with his lantern. "Come on." The boy waited for a nod from his uncle before complying and then shuffled forward to stay by her side.

The light crept across the dark rocky ground and exposed a way between the pools. Lauren put her hand out, and Emre took it, giving it a strong squeeze for good measure. The pair tiptoed forward as the rest of the group took more of a wait-and-see approach. The cavern floor reflected the lantern light and illuminated a good-sized area, including two pools lying directly in their path.

"It must be hollow," Lauren said after a view of the space between the cavern floor and the surface of the water. "Good god," she said, letting it slip from her mouth. "What could those waterways be used for?"

Emre's face sequenced up at the question as if it smelled terrible. "To get from one place to another," he said matter-of-factly.

The idea struck Lauren with considerable potency. If there were a series of waterways under the rock, who or what would use them?

Their progress brought them to the foot of the life-sized idol carving, interrupting her darkening thoughts. The black stone statuette stood several feet taller than Lauren's five foot three, and the full sight of it brought on a measure of repugnance. Detailed runic lines marked the rock from the base up to the torso. Multiple sets of arms lined either side of the chest, but the head of the thing was most vile.

Lauren involuntarily recoiled as she gazed at the monstrosity. The enormous mouth split wide open, exposing detailed rows of jagged teeth throughout. Dozens of writhing tentacles reached out from the gap, frozen in the air above the figure. The full view was enough for Lauren and Emre to look away.

"What is it?" Emre asked with bated breath.

Lauren's mouth opened, but she realized that she was not sure what she was looking at.

"A god."

Professor Markinson's response caused Lauren and Emre to leap forward, nearly slamming into the figure's base in the process. She spun around, growling directly in the professor's face.

"What in the hell is wrong with you?" she snapped. "This isn't the place to go around sneaking up on someone." The look in the professor's frightened eyes told her that he got the point. Lauren was glad she had decided to put her gun away, or she bet the old man would have a bullet in him. "What god?"

Professor Markinson gathered himself as the outline of Ahmed and Alex hardened in the light as they walked up behind him.

"It's not one I've ever seen," Alex said, studying the larger version of the idol.

The professor shook his head as he took a step closer, being careful to avoid the pools on either side. "I'm not certain," he said and then removed a small notebook from the inside pocket of his jacket. "Maybe…"

Lauren peeked at the pages of the pad as he thumbed through it. Handwritten notes covered each page, some with sketches of figures as terrifying as the one directly in front of them. The sudden recognition of his interests brought with it a sizeable amount of distrust. The professor leered at her over the edge of the book and promptly turned away.

She kept her eyes on him as he continued to look from page to page. A delighted admiration flashed across his face, and he closed the book and put it away without a word. Lauren waited for him to speak, but he kept quiet. His gaze walked over the figure with renewed interest.

Lauren waited as long as she could stand it. "Well? Don't keep us in suspense."

The professor looked at her as if he did not have the slightest idea what she was saying. "Never seen it before."

Lauren was speechless. She was positive the man was lying to her face. Another squeeze on her hand told her Emre had probably sensed that very same thing. She took a deep breath and tried to get past the deception, but Ahmed beat her to it.

"It does not matter," he said. "None of this," he motioned at the figure, "matters to me, and it should not matter to you." He faced the professor. "We must get to the cavern wall and work our way around. If there's a way out of here, that's where it's going to be."

He was moving before he finished the last word. Emre walked after him, pulling on Lauren's arm as he went. She looked back to make sure the professor and Alex were coming and caught the two sharing a few whispered words. They both glanced up at her with renewed fear in their eyes. Something about the look on their faces was more disturbing than beholding the figure itself.

"More of them."

Ahmed's announcement pulled Lauren around. The big man stopped ahead of her. Emre's lantern light revealed another series of pools in the cavern floor and several more figures positioned throughout the open ground. The details were difficult to make out, but it was apparent they were all different from the first statue, though no less disturbing.

Lauren hardened her mind on finding the surrounding barrier and using it to look for an opening back into the city. She took a single step when the light reflected off something as it moved out from behind one of the carved figures then stepped back. The light juddered and then centered on the stature. Emre tried to continue walking, but Lauren did not move, yanking the boy backward.

"Right there," she said and then drew her gun.

The sight of the weapon brought everyone to a halt. Ahmed spun around and focused his gun on the center of the statue.

"What?" he demanded, "What did you see?"

"I'm not sure," she admitted. "It's behind that idol."

"You are sure?"

Lauren nodded with determination. "You bet your ass."

Ahmed slid out away from the others, trying to avoid falling into one of the pools and keeping his gun trained on the statue simultaneously. Lauren waited until Alex turned his flashlight on the statue before she dared to move. They spread out as a group, with Professor Markinson on one end and Ahmed on the other. The remaining lights focused on the idol, lighting it up entirely. The entire scene froze as no one dared move once they were in place.

Lauren watched the sight on the barrel of her gun. She shook as the tension built. She was sure she had seen something, but the painfully long pause made her question her sanity. A glimmer from behind the idol reconfirmed her thought.

"There," she shouted, nearly dropping her weapon in the process.

It was a hand or at least five fingers, but the similarities between it and the onlookers stopped there. The light revealed a blue-green skin that glistened as it stretched. The gangly digits were at least twice the length of a man's, ending more of a point than a rounded tip. The hand wrapped around one of the idol's arms and then stiffened.

Lauren slid an eye toward Ahmed. He was in a firing stance, both arms out in front, his hands gripping his gun. Emre was between her and his uncle. The boy's frantic eyes remained on the idol. Lauren thought the boy might start crying at any second. She did not have time to consider the others.

"It's moving."

Emre's frightened announcement drew her back to the idol. The hand itself was not moving, but the rest of the owner slid out into the light. It was a humanoid in that it had arms and legs. The light exposed the blue-green skin, which was covered in what could only be described as scales. It was lanky at the chest and shoulders and stood on muscular legs that ended at elongated feet.

The onset of terror-filled Lauren as she set her gaze on the face of the wretched thing. Drawn to eyes three times the size of her own, she found a milky white swirl absent of any human quality. A jutting forehead fronted its hairless skull. There was no sign of ears or a nose except for a deep hole between its eyes. An under bitten jaw hung open at a small mouth filled with jagged teeth that gave a hint of the thing's taste for meat.

"Professor?"

Alex's plea sounded like a frightened child. Lauren did not take her eyes off the thing until she heard the yelp that followed the plea. A loud splash followed Alex's squeal. A sudden chill struck her as water-soaked the side of her pants. She turned to find Alex disappearing beneath the surface of the nearest pool.

"Help."

Professor Markinson was already down on his knees at the edge of the pool, grabbing at his assistant. Alex lashed about violently before dropping down beneath the surface. She dropped her gun on the cavern floor and reached out for him. The freezing water stung her skin as her hand plunged under. She grabbed a firm hold of something and pulled. Alex burst up through the water with a monstrous gasp. Professor Markinson seized his arm, and he and Lauren pulled Alex out of the pool. Lauren did not wait to see if he was breathing. She picked her gun up and spun toward the idol, but the creature was gone.

"Where'd it go?" she asked, peering at Ahmed. "Did you see it move?"

The guide sidestepped toward her, never taking his aim off the direction of the statue. Emre was already at her side, and the boy answered for his uncle.

"I turned around when I heard the scream. It was gone when I brought the light back around."

Lauren and Ahmed stepped forward together. Emre laid his lantern down next to Alex before joining them. They crept forward with guns at the ready. A cough from Alex said he was going to live, but that was the least of Lauren's concerns. She and Ahmed spread out as they neared the idol. They were a few steps away from it when it became obvious that whatever they saw was gone. A small pool on the floor behind the idol hinted at where the creature went.

"That settles it," Lauren said, lowering her weapon. "We are not down here alone." Something about admitting the fact aloud made the idea more startling. She looked around at the group with renewed bewilderment. "What the hell was that?" The question, she knew, was a valid one, although she also figured no one would be able to provide an acceptable answer.

Alex was upon his knees, every part of him soaked to the bone. Professor Markinson stood next to his assistant, staring back at her. Lauren felt a strong urge to punch him square in the gut, but she knew it would not do her much good. Any dark secrets he was keeping from the rest of the group would probably not help escape Morgainok. She tried to calm herself as she urged the others to gather around Alex. Lauren was unable to stop her mouth before her words came out.

"You're a son of a bitch," she said, looking directly at the professor. The assertion came out harsher than she had intended, but it felt good getting it out in the open. "We're going to die down here, eaten by some—" she looked back at the dim outline of the idol behind them "—I do not even know what to call it, and I can't help feeling this is all somehow your fault." She paused to allow the man a chance to defend himself, but she swore that if he said anything about not believing there was something else down in that cavern with them, she was going to kick him between the legs.

The professor appeared to sense the possibility of confrontation because he had his hands up in defense before she finished. Lauren waited for a reply, but she caught sight of something she had not seen before. The smug look of superiority had vanished from the professor's face. The expression that replaced the usual air about him was plain and simple: fear. His countenance caused her anger to subside if only a little.

"I didn't…" he muttered to himself before finally looking her in the eyes. "I did not know."

Lauren's scowl softened. No matter how much blame the man deserved, he was stuck as much as any of them. She reminded herself that none of it mattered anyway. Whether she wanted to kick his ass or not, it would not do any good unless they found a way out. She looked from Alex's shivering face to Ahmed's determined stare.

"Lead the way."

5

The sudden realization that someone or something still lurked within the dark city of Morgainok was petrifying. The professor's logical mind could not produce a sound explanation, and the exercise was debilitating for him. He had nearly convinced himself that the drumbeats came from some natural phenomenon, but he could not deny the face of the thing behind the idol. It was not human, at least not in any form he recognized.

A loud thud interrupted his internal debate. A series of hits followed the first until a renewed wave of the beating drums washed over the wall surrounding the open space. It was not the resuming beat that increased the group's terror, but the recognition by all at how close they were. Alex had lost his flashlight in his dip in the pool, not to mention his pack and the remainder of his gear, leaving Emre's lantern as the only source of light. Ahmed did not wait for direction.

"Come, we must go."

They moved in a line, with Ahmed guiding them out front. Emre offered up his lantern, and Professor Markinson took it, trailing the formation. Alex sloshed along in front of him, leaving his wet prints along the way. The professor held the lantern up near his face, but the dying light only produced enough power to see a stone's throw in any direction. The professor did not realize the group had come to a stop until he stepped on the back of Alex's boot.

"What is it?" he whispered. "Why are we stopped?"

Alex shrugged. The professor pushed past him, and it took a few strides to realize the rest of the group had gotten further ahead. The glow of the lantern slid off the ground and up the back of the three figures, looking at something beyond the light. He followed Lauren's stare to several of the tall, carved idols lined up near what appeared to be an opening leading into the dark city walkways.

"What is the problem?" the professor asked, and the ridiculousness of the question nearly made him laugh. He thought to rephrase the inquiry, but Ahmed provided an answer.

"It moved."

The simple statement brought with it a considerable amount of power. Professor Markinson looked at the life-sized statues with renewed interest. He scanned the edges of each of the more than half-dozen figures before he fully understood. Ahmed did not mean something moved out from beyond the carvings; he meant the *idol* moved. The professor was convinced that the two statues closest to the exit shifted in unison, and then each took a step toward the group. His response came from somewhere deep within his gut.

"Run."

The professor was frantic, launching off on his own with little concern for who or what was around him. It was only after he nearly plunged into one of the countless pools that he had enough wherewithal to use his lantern to help guide him. He screamed as he ran, unable to calm himself enough to stop. He was out of breath when he finally slowed enough to look back for the others.

The sinister beating drums continued, now seemingly whipped into a frenzy by the chase. The shock of realizing he was alone hit the professor all at once. The shaking circle of light gave away his fear as he fought the urge to call out. A scream from somewhere beyond his illumination was enough to break him.

"Alex." He waited for a response that did not come. "Ahmed?"

The professor backed away and stumbled. He pressed his hand behind him in time to catch himself on the cold stone wall. There was some solace in recognizing the barrier around the open space. He kept a hand on the wall and forced himself to walk. Another yell rang out from the darkness. Lauren, he thought, but he could not be certain. The sound of the drums rose all around him, and his body shook with intensity to match it.

He counted his steps aloud, if for no other reason than to hear his voice break the beating thumps. His chest swelled as his heart thundered beneath the skin. Another step and the light crossed an opening in the wall. The break in the barrier was enough to get him to move faster. Two more steps, he was out of the open area and again in between the bizarre structures lining the city walkway. A glance at the open area brought with it a heart-stopping view as a hand reached out for him. The professor sprinted forward before recognition of the voice from the darkness took hold.

"Professor, wait."

Alex was still shivering when he stepped into the soft glow of the lantern. He wrapped his arms around his chest as the professor took the entire picture in.

"Where is everyone else?" the professor asked, peering past him.

Alex shook his head but did not respond. Professor Markinson considered what to do next when a sudden realization came over him. The drums had stopped. Alex's head shot up as the recognition appeared to set in.

"Ahmed?" The professor's whispered call felt like a shout in the haunting silence. "Lauren?"

They held their place for a painfully long time before they received a response.

"Help."

The call was faint and too distant to be precise, but the accent gave Ahmed away. Professor Markinson grabbed Alex and pulled him close. He aimed them toward the center of the opening in the wall and held the lantern out in front.

"We can't go back in there," Alex said.

The professor considered their situation. He did not fancy himself as a hero, but he was a survivor, and the chances of him and Alex getting out of Morgainok alone were slim. The decision was made for him, and he took credit as best he could.

"We're going to get them," he said.

Alex's expression soured, but he did not object. His shivering increased as he walked, both of them side by side, through the entrance and into the open space. The professor performed a mental check of everything in his backpack and stopped at the first item he felt might protect him. He was down on one knee a second later, freeing the small pick he used to chip away at dirt and rock. The miniature nature of the tool did not improve his sense of security, but he was glad to have something in his hand to swing.

"This is crazy," Alex said under his breath and then repeated louder, "This is crazy."

"Shut up," the professor responded. "Do you think you can lead us out of here?"

Alex started to respond when an abrupt *ah-ha* awareness crossed his face. The professor took it to mean they agreed. The glowing lantern light exposed the edge of a pool, and the mere sight of the water brought the duo to a halt. Professor Markinson had a haunting vision of the creatures posing as idols. Another call from the darkness joined the vision.

"Help me."

Ahmed was close, and the professor caught enough of his plea to hold the direction. They sidestepped the pool and continued forward. It was not long before a low moan directed them to their guide. He lay on the ground on his back, his eyes closed, and a whispering stream of groans slipping from his lips.

"Give him water," the professor said as he set the lantern down and knelt at Ahmed's side. "Can you hear me?" he asked, placing his hand on his chest. Alex took the professor's canteen and tried to get Ahmed to drink. "Do you know where Lauren is?" There was no response from Ahmed to either the question or the edge of the canteen pressed against his lips. "Where is Emre?"

The reaction to his nephew's name was immediate and violent.

Ahmed sat up and did so with enough force to knock the professor back. The canteen went flying and smacked Alex in the chest.

"Emre," Ahmed shouted.

Professor Markinson grabbed his shoulder to keep him from standing and managed to get back up on his knees in the process. Ahmed turned to face the professor with a profound look of terror.

"Where are they?" the professor asked.

It took a second for Ahmed to recognize the faces in front of him. He shook his head slowly and then looked out at the darkness beyond the light.

"I do not know," Ahmed said. "I had his hand." He looked at his palm, bewildered by it. "He slipped away."

The professor glanced around with renewed interest. He had a sudden recognition that he was not going to be able to get Ahmed to help them escape without his nephew. His eyes picked out the soft light within the rock of the surrounding city structures. He was drawn to the brightest distant point.

"The pyramid," he said, drawing in both Ahmed and Alex. "They'll make their way to the pyramid."

"Why would they do that?" Alex asked. "They're probably de—"

The professor cut him off. "It is the most visible point," he said and then stood up and offered Ahmed his hand. "That is where I would go if I were lost." He was unsure if he believed what he was saying, but he was hedging his bet. He needed Ahmed to guide them, and he did not want to waste unnecessary time hunting around Morgainok for someone who was dead or would be soon. His plan involved finding a way out and returning with a sizable force of his own to take full credit for discovering the nefarious city of legend.

He helped Ahmed stand. The bigger man grabbed the lamp as he got to his feet, and the light shifted, revealing another figure beyond where they found him. The professor involuntarily shook his head as he leaned in closer for a look. The scaly hide of the thing gave it away, and the recognition caused Professor Markinson to quiver.

"My God," Alex said as he took a step toward it. "He killed it."

The declaration led the professor's focus to a long gash in the creature's side and a knife lying on the ground next to the body. A deep blue liquid dripped from the wound, matched by a sizable stain still on the blade. All three men stood over it, and the lantern allowed them to take in the full sight in one glimpse. It was far taller than the professor imagined, guessing it at least seven feet.

"It must come up out of the water," Alex said and then pointed. "It has some kind of gills."

Small slits lined the side of its head behind two orifices on either side. Its mouth hung open at a wide angle, revealing several uneven rows of teeth, lining the gap down to its throat.

"I bet this would be worth a pretty penny," Alex said.

Professor Markinson glared at him. "You will keep your mouth shut about everything we've seen," he said. "When we get out." He corrected himself, "If we get out of here, you will not tell a soul what we've discovered." The professor would not allow his assistant to destroy what could be the pinnacle of his professional life.

"It grabbed me in the dark," Ahmed said, pulling the professor back to the moment. "I tried to keep a hold of Emre, but that thing wrapped its hand around my arm and tried to drag me down into the water." He shook his head as he came to terms with what was going on. "I had to let him go," he explained. "I thought it was going to kill me, and I did not want to pull Emre down with me."

Professor Markinson only vaguely heard Ahmed's description of the attack. His mind fixed on the simple fact that whatever the aquatic being was, there were most definitely more of them. More importantly, he wanted to ensure he could survive long enough to escape from Morgainok. The professor knew Ahmed was the key to his survival; Alex was expendable, on the other hand.

"We will look for them, of course," the professor said, sensing what he needed to say to sway the guide into action. "We must not call out," he added. "We will attract those things to us."

There was a mutual nodding at the wisdom of the idea, and the refocus appeared to work. Ahmed steadied himself.

"We found the opening over there," Alex pointed.

Ahmed's eyes looked out at the pyramid, and the awful thing glimmered in the distance. It took a moment for all of them to realize the flickering light was not coming from the unnamed substance hidden within the rock. Alex formed the word before the others.

"Fire."

The sight was clear, and it pointed to an indisputable fact.

"There are more than just those things down here in the dark city," Ahmed announced. "Much more than I think you ever imagined." He glanced at the professor, who offered only a nod in response. "We have awoken a long-forgotten evil. And now it looks for us in the dark."

The professor wanted to brush off his remarks, but a lingering fear kept him from it. There was much more to Morgainok. The fires hinted at a way out of the cavern near the pyramid. It also meant the pyramid was the one place they did not want to go. He would have to appease Ahmed's concerns before he would help them escape. It did not matter to him if Emre was alive or dead. Lucky for the professor, Ahmed came up with a solution they could mutually accept.

"We will work our way around the outside of this open area," he said, whispering as if the distant fires could hear him. "There may be other exits." He nodded to himself for reassurance. "And perhaps Emre and Ms. Miller are waiting there for us to find them." He waited for the professor and Alex to nod their agreement. "Then we will move on."

Professor Markinson did not want to waste time retracing their steps, but he knew he did not have the advantage to force the issue. He begrudgingly followed the guide as they headed for the exit point. They found the gap in the surrounding wall and then stepped out on the dark city walkway, greeted by a familiar haunt. The drums resumed at a frantic pace, pushing between the odd structures. The initial blast froze the trio in place, but the overwhelming fear was too much to bear. They sprang forward with terror in their hearts. The drums edged closer, seemingly from around every corner as if the lurking beasts were nipping at their heels.

6

Lauren heard the drums. She stood still for a long time; one hand wrapped firmly around her pistol grip and the other around Emre's wrist. Neither she nor Emre knew what those things were near the pools. They were, however, sure they wanted to get away from them as quickly as possible.

The professor's shout to run did not come with directions. In the chaos that followed, Lauren found herself alone. She and Emre slammed into one another a short time later, and the evidence of their collision still pounded on the side of her head. She took it upon herself to lead the boy, and they found their way back out into the city walkways a short time later.

"It's getting closer."

Lauren shushed Emre but acknowledged his excited utterance. The damn drums were much closer, and the overwhelming sound made it nearly impossible to determine which way they were coming from. The fear that proceeded the pounding beat brought with it a sizeable dose of indecision. Lauren was capable of putting aside the fantastic visions of what they had seen if only enough to fool herself, but her experience in the field could not prepare her for the overwhelming sense of dread clinging to her soul.

"Where would Ahmed go?"

Her whispered question had been for herself, but Emre offered up an answer.

"He'd look for me."

She nodded. He was right. Ahmed was a principle-driven man, and there was no way he would willingly leave his nephew down in Morgainok to die. That, of course, assumed Ahmed was still alive himself, and it did not account for what the professor and Alex would rather him do. Lauren pulled Emre in close to give him directions when the beating drums came to an unexpected stop. The two looked around at the pale glow in the rock, more terrified by the haunting silence.

"We cannot sit here and wait," she whispered. "We have to keep moving." His eyes widened at the sound of her decision, and she continued before he could argue with her. "Whoever is beating on those drums is closing in on us, and I, for one, don't want to find out what they mean to do if they find us."

The jolt of his abrupt understanding was enough to get him to hold his tongue. He nodded sluggishly. They had not taken more than a step when a new sound echoed toward them from somewhere up ahead. The footsteps were distinct, slapping the rock as they rushed forward and then stopped. Lauren's eyes had adjusted to the low light enough to see the outline at the end of the walkway where the path split.

Emre reacted first, pulling Lauren with him. He dashed into an opening of one of the bizarre structures lining the footpath and stopped short of falling into a pool in the center of the floor. Lauren pressed her back against the wall adjacent to the opening and aimed her weapon. She reminded herself that Ahmed and the others were out there somewhere, and she did not want to shoot one of them by mistake.

She kept her eyes on the gun's sights. Lauren heard Emre's panting gasps beside her. The boy held his breath every time the footsteps started. The walker was close; Lauren guessed right outside the opening when she got her first glimpse. The shadow slid across the walkway beyond the opening, and the shapes were impossible to piece together.

Lauren held her breath as the thing stepped out in front of the breach. A webbed foot smacked the rock as it touched down, nearly twice the length of a man's. Blue-green scales covered gaunt legs, which rose above the opening. A pair of arms hung low, swinging from side to side as it moved again. Several elongated fingers grasped the edge of the opening, and the movement revealed a second, smaller pair of arms under the first, these ending at pincers.

Emre pushed into her, and Lauren took her eyes off the thing long enough to beg him not to make a sound. She looked back before it stepped past the breach. The slapping movements continued for a minute longer and then went quiet. Lauren's heart thundered beneath her shirt, and she was confident the sound would soon give them away. She scanned the narrow interior of their hiding spot before accepting the truth of the situation.

"Stay here," she whispered and then tried to step away. Lauren paused when Emre would not let her go. She looked back at him, and he shook his head frantically. "I have to." Emre did not stop shaking, but he released his grip on her arm.

Lauren took her eyes off him as she tiptoed forward. She imagined the boy still silently pleading with her. Every fiber within her body wanted to stay put, but she did not want to be cornered. Whatever it was they found down in Morgainok; it was clear that it was hunting them.

She kept her gun out in front of her, managing to hold her nerves in check enough to shoot straight if she had to. Lauren hesitated before the opening, listening for footsteps and leaning slowly forward. The light within the rock was enough to see the details of the surrounding structures, but she would have to step out in the open to view the walkway in either direction.

Lauren took another step, and she cleared the entrance. She felt a sudden pull on the back of her head before she got a full view of the walkway. Emre screamed somewhere behind her as she was lifted off her feet. Lauren fired her gun before she ever got a look at what had hold of her.

A horrific growl announced the thing before the full view of it seized Lauren's heart. A flash of teeth crossed her face. The growl peaked at a high pitch call that echoed in her ears with a painful response. The sound of the gun going off broke through the howl, and Lauren did not realize she shot the creature until it let her go.

A split second after the pain lifted on the back of her head, she slammed into the ground.

Lauren hit the walkway feet first, and her body collapsed, sending her knees directly up under her chin. The impact propelled her head back with enough jarring force to knock her out. A rush of warm blood filled her mouth as she ended up flat on her back. A renewed howl spurred her to action. She made herself stand, and the world wobbled beneath her feet.

"Ms. Miller. Ms. Miller."

She could hear Emre, but she could not see him. Lauren spit out a wad of blood and found the vile creature stomping toward her. She gazed at the horrifying thing in all its glory. The creature towered over her, its arms spread out wide as it took up the entire width of the walkway. An enormous jowl hung open as a series of slithering appendages reached out in the air above its head. Lauren raised her gun to fire.

"No."

Lauren felt the impact in her side as she pulled the trigger. The gun went off the moment she hit the ground. The creature tripped over her and tumbled across the ground. Emre was already up, his hand out, and Lauren realized he had knocked her out of the way of the charging beast.

"Let's go."

Lauren took his hand and was up and moving before she could process where they were going. The sounds of the creature swelled around them. Lauren's vision blurred as she let Emre guide her. She readjusted her grip on the gun, and the terror rising in her chest urged her to turn around and fire again. Lauren fought off the impulse, saving whatever rounds she had left. A flickering light pulled her attention away from the gun, but any hope they would find the rest of their troupe came to a frightful close.

Emre slid to a grinding halt. The sudden stop left Lauren crashing into the boy from behind. The jittering fire centered on the walk-way, the flames exposed to the dark cavernous air. There was no sign of Ahmed, Alex, or Professor Markinson. They were primar-ily men, dark-skinned, shaven heads, and scarcely clothed, all of them glaring back at the woman and boy with death in their eyes. Lauren gawked over Emre's shoulder, bewildered by the sight. The boy's body trembled against hers, and the recognition increased her dread tenfold. The mass started forward in silence in stark contrast to the blaring creature rushing up from behind.

"Ms. Miller, please."

Emre tugged on her hand as he fell to his knees. A quick scan un-covered their only chance at escape. She dashed through the open-ing of the closest structure, pulling Emre back to his feet as she went. The move produced an eruption of shouts from the group. Lauren and Emre found themselves standing at the edge of a pool, looking across at a familiar view. An assortment of tables lined the far wall, sitting beneath an ascending set of spikes.

"We have to climb," she said as she started for the wall.

"We'll be trapped up there," Emre countered.

Lauren pleaded with him. "They can't all get up there," she said. "And more importantly, that thing won't fit."

The explanation was enough to get the boy's legs moving again. They were midway to the top of the narrowing structure when the first of the mob burst in through the opening.

"Don't look down," Lauren exclaimed. A second glance revealed the entire floor space filled with figures, several of which had begun to climb. "Get to the top and try and lift yourself out into the open."

Emre was ahead of her. The boy's spry movements made easy work of the strenuous climb. He reached the gap in the ceiling and disappeared a moment later. A chorus of unintelligible shouts filled the interior of the structure, followed by a booming roar.

Lauren did not need to look to know what was happening. She grabbed a glimpse once she reached the hole in the ceiling and saw the terrible creature lashing its gangly arms through the ground floor opening.

"Take my hand."

Emre grabbed hold of her and pulled. The enormity of the cavern struck her the moment she stepped out onto the structure's roof. Towering edifices lined the city around them, none as impressive as the mighty pyramid rising up at the heart of it all. Lauren leaned over the hole in the roof and aimed at the first of the tribal men climbing after them.

"We can jump," Emre said with a noticeable dose of hope. "I'll go first."

"Wait—"

Lauren turned in time to see the boy mid-air, out in the expanse between their roof and the next. Emre hit the rocky surface with considerable skill, stopping in a perfect landing. He called back to her as he waved her over.

"Hurry," he said. "I will catch you."

Closer inspection revealed the next landing was lower than their rooftop escape. Lauren gauged the distance, stalling as she tried to talk herself into jumping.

"Hurry."

"Give me a second," she shouted, brushing him off with a swipe of her hand. She glanced down at the walkway and regretted it the instant her eyes found the ground. "Oh, God."

A pair of hands reaching up through the hole in the ceiling gave her all the motivation she needed. Lauren took a step back before launching herself across the open space. She could not control the panic in her gut, which showed itself in a shrilling scream. Lauren did not realize that the angle of her jump was off until she was midway between the two rooftops. The recognition struck home when a single boot tapped the landing spot, and her momentum kept her moving forward. A flash of her impending death exploded in her mind, and only Emre's quick action kept it from becoming a reality.

A hard grab froze Lauren in place, leaning out over the edge of the building with one foot dangling in the open space. Emre's grunt signaled his attempt to save her. The boy's strength was enough to pull her back, and she did not breathe again until she had both feet safely planted on the rooftop. Lauren spun around and wrapped her arms around Emre, forgetting for the briefest moment that a tribe of people was chasing after them, not to mention some unholy creature she would not dare attempt to name.

"They are coming up."

Emre's warning brought Lauren back to the present. She followed his extended hand to the hole in the roof of the building they escaped. The first two figures were already preparing to follow Lauren's example while several more fought to push through the breach. Lauren's panicked scan revealed the next structure over was several stories higher, leaving a single option.

"We have to climb down," she said, piecing the plan together in her mind. "But we can't go down the inside."

She motioned at the back of the structure and urged Emre to start his descent. There was not much time for planning, but her gut told her they would be cornered if they climbed down the interior of the tower. The tribal mass, as well as the howling thing, would meet them on the street below. Climbing down the backside of the tower would force the pursuers to either follow or find a way around to an adjacent walkway.

Emre's head disappeared beneath the edge of the roof before Lauren knew it. She grabbed a quick handhold and tried to keep up. The last view of the rooftop saw the first tribesman miss the leap between the buildings. He smacked the lip of the roof at the waist and then fell back. He disappeared over the side, screaming all the way down. Several shrieks followed the first jumper, but Lauren kept her eyes on the climb. She felt Emre's hands on her legs before she realized they had reached the ground.

"Which way?" Emre asked, his head jerking from one side of the walkway to the other.

In truth, Lauren had no idea which way to go. She also had no idea how they ever hoped to escape the dark city. Lauren focused on the one thing she could make out in the distant light. The pyramid called her like a beacon in the night, but she did not know if it was a hope for safety or the flame for the moth. She pointed out the marker before the words reached her lips.

"We're going to try and get to the pyramid."

Emre's muted response was easy to decipher. The boy was terrified, and he did not attempt to hide it. "That is an evil place," he said, paraphrasing his uncle's words. "We mustn't."

Lauren was out of options. She placed both hands on Emre's face and made him look her in the eyes. All she had was honesty. He would have to accept it.

"I do not know what we're supposed to do," she admitted. "But we're together, and we have to be strong for one another."

Emre was quiet for an instant longer, and then the tension in his face softened as he nodded. "Okay." He gazed back at the distant pyramid. "Let's go."

7

The sound of the drums disappeared as quickly as they had arrived. Professor Markinson never moved with his feet seemingly stuck to the stone walkway. Several haunting sounds blared out from nearby in no discernable order. A ferocious howl shook the professor to the core, but gunshots filled him with dread. Apparently, the two missing members of their expedition had survived their separation from the group, or Lauren at the least. The professor feared she would come face to face with whatever was howling in the dark, and he doubted very much that there was a good reason to go searching for her now.

"It was that way," Ahmed said before starting again. "We must hurry if we have any hope of helping them."

Alex grabbed the man by his sizable forearm and tried to stop him. "That...that thing, whatever it was," Alex said. "It got them."

Ahmed yanked his arm away from Alex's grasp. "You do not know that."

Alex stared at the professor in a silent plea for help. Professor Markinson thought to let Ahmed go, but a nagging feeling told him they would not survive without him.

"If they are alive," the professor said, "they're on the run from whatever it was we heard."

The announcement was enough to get Ahmed to pause, but he did not turn around. "We must go to where they're heading and not waste our time or risk our lives trying to find out where they were."

There appeared to be enough sense in what he was saying to get Ahmed to consider it. The professor watched the bigger man take a deep breath before finally facing them.

"The pyramid," Ahmed said plainly, and Professor Markinson nodded. "And you think our escape lies somewhere near that damned construction?"

The professor took a few strides forward to close the gap between them and pulled Alex with him as he passed. "I didn't say that."

"Then how is that any safer than running around the city?" Ahmed asked.

"I can't promise safety," the professor said and then urged the both of them to move. "All I can say is it is a logical gathering point, for us, as well as," he paused, "anything else roaming the streets of Morgainok."

Alex's head popped up. "That sounds more like a reason why we shouldn't go there."

The response froze the professor in his tracks. Alex was correct. A sudden spark of light highlighted the point. All eyes went to the pyramid structure, and another light followed the first glow. Several fires sprang to life along the face of the distant construction, outshining the pale light hidden within the rock.

The professor's response slipped out without much thought. "Well then, that is peculiar indeed."

He decided the statement was woefully underwhelming for the situation.

"And you still want to go there?" Alex asked, pressing the issue.

Professor Markinson nodded, unsure that he believed it.

Ahmed was more assertive. "I will go there," he said. "I must find Emre."

Alex threw his hands up in defeat. "Fine then."

◆

The professor would have preferred to take the most direct route through the dark city, but Ahmed would not have it. He might have been hellbent on finding his nephew, but he was determined to be as cautious as possible along the way. Ahmed led them through the walkways between the rising structures toward the furthest side of the enormous cavern. Professor Markinson thought Morgainok might go on forever; however, a sheer wall, similar to the one they used to climb down into the city, awaited them.

"We are not climbing to that thing," Alex said, his eyes running along the edge of a prominent outcropping several stories up. "At least not without proper gear."

The professor was not certain Alex's deduction was correct. If it were a life or death situation, which he was sure their current predicament counted as, they might be able to risk the dangerous climb. There was no guarantee the ledge above acted as an entrance to another system of caves, but he had a fair guess. The professor watched Ahmed as he studied the opportunity.

"What do you think?"

Ahmed put his hands on his hips, his eyes still on the outcropping. He finally sighed and then offered up his opinion.

"If we had to," he said, glancing at Alex and then the professor. "We could climb it." He paused and made sure the professor was looking directly at him. "We could all climb it."

Professor Markinson understood his point. Ahmed would not make any attempts until he either held Emre or knew that the boy was dead. The professor figured as much. That, however, did not mean he or Alex had to be willing to make the same sacrifice. The professor was honest with himself; he would not have a problem leaving Emre or Lauren behind if needed.

"Let's keep moving," Ahmed said. He took a few steps before realizing neither the professor nor Alex had moved.

Alex looked at the professor, and the two silently understood the internal debate. If Ahmed had not gotten the hint, he soon would.

"That could be the only way out of here," the professor said.

Ahmed stomped toward them, and for a second, the professor

thought he might have to defend himself. Ahmed stopped a foot from his face.

"You are a coward."

The shout startled the professor, and he stumbled backward and tripped. His backside hit the ground before he realized what had happened.

"You want to go?" Ahmed continued and turned his glare on Alex and then pointed up at the outcropping. "Then go. But you go alone." He spun on his heels and stormed off.

Alex leaned in close to the professor and whispered, "He has most of the remaining gear in his backpack."

Professor Markinson nodded. "I'm not sure we would like his response if we asked him to leave it behind."

They watched Ahmed as he walked away, each torn with whether or not they should run after him.

"We know this place," the professor said. "Or at least we know if we stick to the edge of the cavern, we could find it again." He glanced at the ledge. "And the possibility does exist that there is a safer way out."

"And there is also the possibility that one of those things could find us," Alex retorted.

The professor marched after Ahmed, ignoring Alex's reservations. Professor Markinson's decision was clear. "Stay here if you like."

The walkways widened the closer they moved toward the center of the city. The view of the pyramid was unmistakable, the details growing with every step. The firelight was unmistakable, and it soon became evident that there was movement along the face of the grand edifice. Professor Markinson cleared the edge of a long row of structures, and the trio stepped out into a shockingly open view.

The stone floor declined steeply into a vast depression. A tall barrier lined the edge of one side of the impression, blocking access to the edge of the cavern. Ahmed led them to the rim of the bowl, and they peered down at the interior with inexplicable fascination. The light embedded in the rock was on full display. The pale blue lines formed an amazingly intricate depiction. A series of rock formations filled the bottom of the bowl, some no bigger than a shoebox and others more massive than the structures they had already encountered. The lines of light covered nearly every inch of the floor, cascading the glow up into the darkness. Lining walls worked around the bowl in every direction, creating an uncountable number of paths and intersecting walkways.

"What is it?" Alex asked, studying the lines. "A maze?"

Ahmed shrugged off the question, instead focusing on the bowl's rim around the formation.

"We cannot get around it," he said. "We either go down to try and cross through it or go back to look for another way."

They looked at Professor Markinson, and he knew that they wanted him to make the decision. The professor could not hide his archaeological fascination with what they found. His childlike wonderment pushed back the sense of impending doom, if only temporarily. He slid one foot onto the sloping rock and steadied himself.

"Going straight through is the fastest way," he said without much thought. "Careful here."

The professor surprised himself by how quickly the fear controlling his mind slipped into curiosity. He led them down the steep drop at a cautious pace until they reached a place that allowed for more sure-footed steps. They moved forward in a line, pushed in close together, taking in the maze environment as the rock formations rose around them.

A statue of sorts greeted them; the base carved directly out of the floor supporting the rest of the creation. A single rock lay atop the base, oblong through the center and coming to a rounded point on either end. A pair of elongated pieces swept away from the midpoint of the mass, hanging down close to the ground. There was something strangely familiar about the piece, but Professor Markinson could not place it.

"It's a symbolic deity of some sort," Alex said, guessing at its purpose.

The announcement produced a sudden terrifying memory, and all three men took a step back. A sudden urge to run away struck the professor.

"The last idol we came across moved," Ahmed announced, giving words to the feeling crawling through each of their minds.

They held still for a long time. There was a collective sigh from the group before any of them were willing to approach it. The professor hesitated, then reached out and touched one of the extending arms. He found some relief when the cool rock confirmed that it was nothing more than a sculpture.

"NasNoroth."

Alex spit the name out with a wild recognition, and a spark struck Professor Markinson with considerable force. He stepped back again, looking over the idol with renewed fear. NasNoroth was a lead figure within the ancient text of the Cult of the Elder. The professor had never taken the description of the deity to be a literal depiction, but the sculpture fit the words he had read numerous times.

"Unbelievable," he said, shocked at the realization.

Ahmed would not go near it. The guide carefully sidestepped the sculpture and was already on the opposite side, looking at what lay ahead of them. Professor Markinson took one last glance before urging Alex to catch up. The view was surprisingly well lit. The pale lines beneath the rock converged in several places along a series of formations, intensifying the light. The strategically placed formations created defined walkways with tall boundaries along either side.

The first glimpse of the interior of the maze stole the breath from the professor's lungs. The lines of light had a purpose, working out countless ruins along the interior face of the rock. The professor slipped his pack off and laid it on the ground. He rummaged through it, trying to keep one eye on their discovery and one on the contents. He produced the book he sought and handed it over to Alex.

"The heaven opened," the professor said, translating the work by memory. "And fire rained down across the sea." He caught sight of Ahmed walking away and lost his place. "Hold on now." Ahmed kept going. "Ahmed, where are you going?"

Ahmed stopped. His hand went to his hip as he tapped his boot on the ground. He shook his head before acknowledging Professor Markinson. "I don't care about this," he said, motioning at the ruins. "I don't care about any of it. This is an evil thing you seek to know, and I will not hear a word of it." He turned his shoulder and revealed the gun in his hand. "Let's go now." He urged them to move with a wave of the weapon, and for the first time, the professor took it as a threat. "No more of this," he warned.

The professor glanced at Alex and found his hands up in defense. Ahmed nodded to himself and then slid the gun into his waist. He was already several steps away before Alex found the nerve to speak.

"You think he would hurt us?" he asked.

The professor picked his bag up off the ground and took the book from Alex. "No," he replied and shook his head. "I think he is scared, nearly as scared as us." They started after Ahmed. "And most important, he still believes there's a chance he can save his nephew."

"That's crazy," Alex said. "He's surely dead, and Lauren too."

The coldness of the response was surprising even for Alex.

"Be that as it may," the professor said, tightening the straps on his pack, "we won't get out of here until he's convinced."

Alex mumbled something to himself before replying. "And that might be the death of us too."

◆

The central path continued straight through the maze. Professor Markinson gleaned several passages from the ruins, never stopping long enough to draw Ahmed's ire. The entire formation was set up like a historical record. He imagined the countless side passages worked as topical splits, representing the other deities that the original people of Morgainok worshiped. The central path was dedicated to NasNoroth, the apparent ruling divine being. The professor continued on the forced march until they reached the very center of the depression, and the view brought him, Alex, and Ahmed to a standstill.

The walkway opened to a perfectly circular space. The light in the walls was at its brightest along the sides facing the center. Drawings of incredible detail replaced the carved records. Professor Markinson looked to Ahmed, silently asking for permission to inspect what they found. The guide nodded and motioned for the professor to lead. They stood side by side looking over the find, and the careful review brought with it a renewed sense of dread. A majority of the scenes depicted sacrificial ceremonies, most centered on the pyramid.

The mural shifted near the wall's midpoint to a scene portraying what appeared to be the very maze they were standing in. There was a moment of odd recognition for Professor Markinson, followed quickly by deep concern. Several large creatures stalking the walkways highlighted the scene on the wall. The view focused on a pair of stick figures positioned in the circular center point of the maze. An echoing cry broke the professor's moment of recognition.

"What was that?" Alex asked as he spun around, attempting to look in every direction at once. "It's over there, I think."

Ahmed pointed in the opposite direction. "No, there."

The professor came to the answer after another glance at the mural. "They're closing off the exits," he said, and his announcement drew in the terrified eyes of both Alex and Ahmed. Professor Markinson felt sick. His legs wobbled beneath him, and for a moment, he thought he might collapse. "They," he repeated as if the word had a much deeper meaning.

Alex grabbed his arm. "What do you mean?"

The professor could not force himself to speak. He pointed at the mural and stumbled back. Alex moved in close to the wall with Ahmed peering over his shoulder. The two looked long enough to get a general idea. They ended up in the center of the circular room staring at one another.

"We will use the carvings to figure a way out," Ahmed announced. "We will climb the walls and get the hell out of here."

Something deep within the professor smothered his confidence. His desperation was quickly acknowledged from somewhere within the maze. A blaring growl washed over the top of the surrounding formations, bringing with it an unimaginable panic. The professor shook at the sound, then staggered and fell. An answering call followed the first growl, this one in a deeper bellowing tone.

Ahmed checked his remaining rounds and readied himself. He offered the professor his hand. Professor Markinson peered up at the guide, full of bleakness. Ahmed glanced at Alex before turning to leave. His words cut to the point.

"Stay here and die if you like," he said. "They'll have to catch me first."

8

Morgainok was coming alive. Lauren and Emre ran wildly at times and then huddled in the shadows of the bizarre structures when their pursuers drew close. There was no real purpose in their plan, and Lauren knew it. Intentionally ignoring their desperation, she feared she might lose her mind if she accepted it. Lauren was determined to keep a goal ahead of them, and for the moment, that goal was the pyramid structure.

"We must stop," Emre said, and his raspy voice hinted at the burning in his lungs. "I have to rest."

Lauren was not far behind him. Her legs ached from the constant push, and she could barely breathe in enough air to keep herself going. She offered a nod, unable to get the words out to accept his plea. They settled on the backside of a lofty tower, positioned at a crossroads of the walkways.

Shadows shifted out in front of them. There was no way to be sure which direction their pursuers were coming. The distant beating drums wrapped around them, washing between the structures from every direction at once. An occasional squeal rose above the noise echoing off the stone walls.

"We can't wait here very long," Lauren said. She patted Emre on the back, and the boy silently bobbed. "There must be a way out of this godforsaken place."

Emre raised his head. "My uncle will come for us," he said with more confidence than she could imagine. "He will not leave us here to die."

Lauren suppressed a grin. She could not account for his certainty, nor could she use it to smother the doom slowly swallowing her. Instead, she simply nodded and let it go. She figured the hope would keep the boy's legs moving, if only for a while longer.

"Stay close to me," she said and then rechecked her gun. A quick count did not increase the number of remaining rounds. "Here we go."

Lauren slid her backside along the rocky exterior of the structures with one hand aiming the gun in the direction they were going and the other holding on to Emre. Sweat rolled down the side of her face as she tiptoed forward. No matter which way she looked, the sounds of the drums greeted them. She aimed toward the pyramid, damning the consequences. Moreover, the consequences raised their head quickly.

A thunderous shout rose above the drums as a mass of arms and legs poured out into the walkway ahead. Lauren fired two shots before she thought to run. One of the dark-skinned men clutched his chest as blood spurt from his neck and sprayed the crowd. A naked woman fell beside him, grabbing at her gut, and the throng trampled her as they raced forward.

Lauren ran between two towers, pulling Emre behind her. The boy picked up speed quickly and was out in front of her before she realized it. He took hold of her arm with a powerful clamp and forced her to match his strides. The beating of the drums intensified, joined by a chorus of jeers and screams from the trailing mob.

One blind turn led to another, and before Lauren knew it, the view of the pyramid was lost somewhere among the countless structures around them. A flurry of light sparked to life on either side of the walkway. Torchlight sprang through the narrow passages between the buildings, sending long shadows reaching out from the dark. Emre galloped like a young buck, and Lauren nearly tumbled several times before her arm slipped from the boy's tight grip. Emre slid to a stop and spun around.

"I can't breathe," Lauren said, clutching her side.

Emre took her hand and pulled. He could not form words between his gasps, but he was determined to keep them moving. The sounds of the mob grew nearer with every breath. Lauren forced herself to take a step.

"There is something up ahead," Emre said after they crossed between two larger structures. "Water?"

The one-word question helped Lauren focus her ears. She picked out the subtle sound of rushing water between the steady beats of the ghastly drums. They continued forward and stumbled across the source of the sound before they realized it. Emre came to a stop at the edge of a substantial drop. Lauren stood next to him, and their eyes studied the churning water beneath their feet.

"It's a river," Emre said, using the only description he could find. He looked away long enough to search out the trailing lines of firelight closing in behind them.

Lauren would have called it a canal of sorts. A perfectly smooth incline on either side of the waterway dug deep into the cavern floor. She did not have the time or scientific curiosity to guess its purpose or the power behind the intense flow. The distance from one side of the embankment to the other gave her great concern that either she or Emre possessed the strength needed to swim across.

"Let's look for another way," she said and then found Emre's gaze behind them. A renewed roar from their pursuers matched the terrified look in his eyes. "Or maybe we don't look a gift horse in the mouth."

Somewhere in her mind, Lauren knew the boy had no idea what the proverb meant. She took a firm grip of his hand and told herself she would have to explain it to him later. One good yank was enough to get Emre to move. Lauren jumped off the edge of the canal and pulled him with her. The duo hit the water a heartbeat apart, and the impact wrenched their hands from one another.

Lauren was unprepared for the intense cold. The darkness swallowed her as she went under the water. The intensity of the flow snapped the clips of her pack. The bag and everything in it was gone in a blink. She thrust her gun into her pants pocket and then kicked with all her might. She burst through the surface in a mad search for Emre.

"Here."

Lauren spun around as a pair of hands grabbed onto her. "Try and swim to the side," she said. The world went by them in a flash. It took her a second to lock onto the familiar glow in the rock. She was terrified once she realized how quickly the current swept them away. "Don't you let go."

Emre did his best to stay afloat. His panic was evident, and Lauren wrapped an arm around him like a rescue swimmer to keep him from going under the water. Her free hand slapped the steep bank after several hard kicks. Emre dragged his shoes along the rock until they slowed enough for him to crawl up onto the sloping rock. Lauren stayed close to him, using his weight to get her up into a sitting position.

"Let's not do that again," Emre said, turning over and taking a seat beside her.

She managed a grin. "Agreed," she said and then scanned the rest of the embankment. The climb up to the edge of the canal would be a difficult one, but she figured they could manage if they went up on their hands and knees. "At least they didn't jump in after us," she said, although there was no way to be sure. The intensity of the waterway drowned out everything else, even the drums. "Come on."

The climb was more difficult than either of them imagined. Several poorly placed hands produced painful slides. Lauren was sure her knees were dotted with blood beneath her pants, and her knuckles were worse off. Emre was up and over the edge quickly and then reached down to help her up. Lauren rolled over onto the flat ground and made sure the gun was still in her pocket. She pulled the weapon out and let it drain. Watching the water drip from the barrel did not give her a warm and fuzzy feeling it would fire again when she needed it to.

Both of them shivered from the cold, their clothes soaked through. Emre got up to his feet and looked down at her. She stood up as the two of them took in their new surroundings. Lauren locked in on the pyramid, stunned by how close they were. It was impossible to process how they had come so far in the dark with the help of the canal. The behemoth loomed beyond a few rows of the dark towering structures that made up the common streets of Morgainok.

"You still want to go there?" Emre asked.

His question was a simple one, but Lauren knew there was much more trepidation beneath the surface of the words.

"The professor will go there," she said, not certain it was a sound enough reason. "Your uncle too," she said to add weight to her logic for Emre's sake as well as her own.

Emre peered down the expansive walkway in both directions and then back to Lauren. The response seemed enough to get the boy to move, but the resolve lasted only a few hesitant steps. A flurry of movement ahead brought his hand up. A single vicious growl replaced the bellowing cries of the mob.

The monstrous thing bound forward from the deep shadows of the buildings at an alarming speed, revealing itself in terrifying glimpses. It reached a midway point between the edge of the canal and towering structures before Lauren moved. Powerful legs shone in the glowing light, reflecting off a slimy film lathered over the creature's blue-black skin. A single protruding eye locked onto the meager targets as a horrific orifice spread open at the center of its angular head.

"Oh God," Lauren muttered as she raised her gun. "Run." She pushed Emre to get him moving. "Go now."

Emre stumbled as he turned. Lauren aimed at the beast trampling toward them. She pulled the trigger to the sound of a dull thud. Several attempts produced the same outcome.

"Damn it."

She turned to run and discovered Emre, only a few steps away. A bright firelight moved toward them around the buildings lining the road. Lauren pushed him to run, and they reached a small space between the edge of the canal and the outer wall of the first structure. The thundering gallop of the gruesome creature barreled down on them from behind, and the engulfing terror flung them directly into the firelight.

A seemingly endless wall of dark faces greeted them on the far side of the building. Lauren thought for a split second to make the jump over the canal's edge back into the frigid waters. She stopped the instant Emre was dragged forward by the crowd. Lauren grabbed hold of his shirt and pulled, but the crowd was too powerful. Emre disappeared into the center of the pack, lost within seconds. Lauren stumbled back and wedged herself in the narrow footpath between the spot where the monstrous beast stomped its hooved feet on the main walkway, and the first of the mob started in toward her from the opposite side.

Lauren did not think about what to do; she simply jumped. Her mind was in flux, preparing for the freezing dip that was to come. Something grabbed hold of her wrist midair, and the sudden jerk on her shoulder nearly pulled the limb out of the socket. Fire erupted under her skin, and Lauren was sure her arm was about to tear away from the rest of her body.

She dangled out over the dark water, swinging back and forth. Lauren looked up and discovered an undulating limb wrapped around her wrist. A line of slimy ooze ran down over her arm as she followed the tentacle back to its source. The beast pulled her toward its gaping mouth in one swift pull. The heat of its foul breath swept around her face as she screamed with all the breath in her lungs.

Lauren lifted the gun without thinking, aiming it directly at the monster's eye. She pulled the trigger, and to her surprise, it fired a single shot. An explosion lit up the darkness as the round tore into the bulbous sphere. A splatter of eye matter smacked Lauren in the face before the tentacle released. She hit the ground feet first, and the impact shot up her spine like a car crash.

The creature blared out a deafening cry, rising on its hind lings. Lauren rolled out of the way a split second before its hooves crashed down onto her chest. She jumped up inches from the edge of the canal. A rising commotion pulled her attention away from the churning waters.

The first wave of figures stepped around the nearest building and headed directly for her. The massive beast heaved a thunderous breath and lunged forward. Lauren was quick enough on her feet to move out of the way. The creature slammed into the men stepping out onto the street, and took a handful of them over the edge of the canal as it came down.

Lauren did not stop moving, driving into a forced run when she was out in the open. Her boots smacked onto the ancient road as she pushed herself far beyond her remaining strength. Panic consumed her mind, leaving a vision of the pyramid as her sole focus. She found the enormous construction towering over the surrounding buildings and raced directly toward it.

An ear-piercing cry rushed up to greet her as she slipped between two towers and popped out on the adjoining path. A sudden burst of light brought her to a standstill. Lauren slowly scanned from left to right, horrified by the countless faces staring back at her. The crowd stood as still as statues, countless figures lining the path on either side.

Lauren brought her gun up, swinging her arm from one edge of the street to the other. Her hands shook as she aimed. An assortment of bone jewelry offset the mix of glistening, naked bodies. A flash of metal blades dotted the hands of several among them. The front lines started forward on cue by some silent command as the heinous drums beat away in the background.

"Stay the hell away from me," Lauren shouted. She pulled the trigger, but nothing happened. She stared down at the sight of her gun as the crowd came within arm's reach. "Son of a—"

She felt them all at once, hands pulling at her from every direction. Lauren tried to fight back but quickly found herself face down on the ground. One hard strike thumped her on the back of the head, and the world spun around her. She was sure she heard Emre scream from somewhere beyond her line of sight, and then everything went dark.

9

"I've got to get out of here."

Professor Markinson ignored Alex's pointless prayer. In truth, the professor was as scared as the young man was, perhaps even more, but his mind was trying to piece together any hope of his survival. He was not able to process any useable plan before Ahmed was on the move. The guide glanced at the intricate design of the maze, carved into the centermost wall. Another series of guttural growls carried over the surrounding barriers, this time noticeably closer to the center.

"There's no time," the professor said as the panic rose to his chest. "We'll be trapped in here."

Alex stumbled as he hiked, attempting to look in every direction at once. He spun around one complete turn before tripping over his feet and landing face-first on the cavern floor. "Crap."

He looked up to reveal a line of blood running down the side of his face from a cut on his brow. Professor Markinson grabbed a handful of Ahmed's shirt and pulled. The last thing he wanted was to be left running for his life alone. His survival instinct told him he needed the local if he hoped to escape if for nothing else, to be an alternate morsel for whatever was currently hunting them for sport. Ahmed yanked himself away with a quick spin.

"Give me your hands," he said. The odd request locked the professor in place. "Like this." He demonstrated by interlocking his fingers and holding them waist-high. "Do it now," he instructed and then glanced at Alex. "Get over here or die alone."

Professor Markinson did as he was told, but he did not get the point of the exercise until Ahmed moved into place. He put one foot on the professor's hands and counted down. Everything clicked for the professor by the time Ahmed got to one. Ahmed went straight up in the air and laid his waist on the top of the wall, pulling himself up in one fluid motion.

"I'm next," Alex said, begging as he attempted to force the professor's hands back into place. "Help me."

Professor Markinson had enough. He grabbed his assistant by the collar and slammed the young man into the wall with enough force to cause his head to smack the stone.

"Get a hold of yourself."

Alex did not speak, glaring back at the professor with sudden hate in his eyes.

Professor Markinson kept hold of Alex, but his focus was on Ahmed standing up on the top of the wall. "What do you see?"

"It's far," Ahmed said in his heavy accent. "There's some sort of river carved into the cavern at the edge of the maze."

Alex whispered a whimpering query. "What's coming for us?"

Ahmed shook his head. "I don't know." He reached down for the professor. "Give me your hand."

Professor Markinson let go of Alex as a vicious snarl burst out of the opening in the wall directly across from them. Alex shoved the professor out of the way and grabbed onto Ahmed with both hands.

"Pull me up."

His feet flailed as Ahmed heaved, and the heel of his boot caught the professor on the nose. Another snarl pumped the blood through his veins at an alarming rate, and the rise in sheer terror matched the pounding beat of the professor's heart. Alex was on top of the wall when the white spots cleared from Professor Markinson's eyes.

"Hurry."

The panic in Ahmed's voice launched the professor into action. He thrust himself upward high enough to catch Ahmed at the elbows. The sudden impact nearly pulled the bigger man off his perch. Ahmed leaned back and steadied himself enough to allow Professor Markinson to climb the rest of the way.

The view from the top of the maze was more mesmerizing than it was below. The entire cavern appeared alive all at once. Sparks of light dotted the darkness throughout the city's streets, and the steady pale glow of the lines embedded in the pyramid intensified all at once. Professor Markinson's mind did not have time to process everything before receiving a shove in the back.

"Jump down and run."

The set of directions from Ahmed were firm and direct. Neither Alex nor the professor needed any additional guidance. The first glimpse of the thing hunting them was enough to keep their mouths shut. It slithered more than walked on an elongated body supported by multiple pairs of legs. They could not see the whole of it at once as sections moved in and out of the shadows with blistering quickness.

A pair of golden eyes sat high atop thin stalks connected to its head. The center of its face was composed of a singular pit. Gleaming rows of teeth moved in a heaving circular pattern as its jaw opened and closed in a rhythmic beat. Another snarl escaped from the depths of the pit in its face, spewing out a line of ooze that covered the ground ahead of its body.

Professor Markinson took a step and missed the top of the wall altogether. He tumbled over the side, which ended in a responding smack that left his legs hanging over him and his neck nearly broken. The sounds of the hunting beast motivated the professor to move despite the intense pain racing up and down his spine. Alex was already moving ahead of him, a trail of whimpering pleas echoing from his mouth with every other step.

"Keep going," Ahmed said before placing the palm of his hand in the center of the professor's back. "Get that fool, and we'll get over the next wall."

A brief thought of leaving Alex behind crossed Professor Markinson's mind, but he surmised the morally compassed Ahmed would never abandon him of his own will. The path turned directly ahead, and Alex was out of view before the professor could catch up with him. Ahmed sped past him, and the two found Alex dangling from the far side wall, scraping the ancient stone with his boots as he frantically attempted the climb on his own.

Ahmed did not waste time; he pressed on Alex's rear end, trying to give him the momentum he needed to finish the ascension. Another roar crawled up from behind them, echoed quickly by a matching call from somewhere deeper in the maze. Alex was up on the wall shouting something over the continuing howl of their pursuers. Professor Markinson processed the young man's ramble as Ahmed helped him climb.

"There's a bridge," he said. "We have to make it."

Professor Markinson did not understand the importance of the bridge nor how it would aid them in their escape. The following panic-stricken announcement bought the internal debate to an end.

"By the gods," Ahmed mumbled, and then his grip slipped from the professor's legs. "It's here."

"Take my hand," Professor Markinson pleaded, his hand outstretched toward Alex. "Grab hold, you bumbling idiot."

A horrific guttural sound washed across the wall, bringing with it a horror like no other. The professor felt the fear so deep in his bones that he nearly let go of the wall. He peered up at Alex as the young man's eyes widened seemingly beyond their limits. His mouth opened to scream, but nothing escaped his lips.

"Grab it."

The professor's words fell on deaf ears. Alex dropped down on the other side of the wall without a second glance at his companions. Professor Markinson flung his leg up and pulled with all his strength. He heard Ahmed screaming wildly somewhere beneath him, followed by a pounding on the ground.

A monstrous growl reverberated through the wall, shaking the professor to his core. Professor Markinson's momentum carried him over the wall. His landing was far better than his first attempt but no less painful to his back. He got up to his feet, fueled by a toxic mix of adrenaline and terror.

"Alex."

His assistant was gone. The professor could not wait for a sign of direction. He was alone for the moment, and a glance confirmed Ahmed was not following him. A grim shout from the guide forced the professor to choose his direction, and he sprinted off with no idea of where he was going.

An intensifying light brought the mighty pyramid to the forefront of the professor's mind. The loathsome monument beamed out of the cavernous dark as if intensifying with every beat of his heart. He locked onto the beacon and drove forward. One turn after another left him hopelessly lost. The professor slid to a stop as recognition grabbed hold. The pathway opened up to a central point in the massive bowl, and Professor Markinson knew he had worked his way back to the site where he, Ahmed, and Alex began their terrifying escape. He noted the central pathway and thought back to Ahmed's advice upon discovering the awful maze.

Going straight through is the fastest way.

A series of yells pulled his attention to the opposite side of the opening. The echo came again, this time with a louder scream. Professor Markinson sprinted out into the open, heading directly toward the main path. He reached the walkway before something lurched out for him from one of the side passages.

The shadow of some two-headed creature pushed away from the darkness and into the pale glow of the surrounding rock. Professor Markinson hollered with such ferocity that his throat burned beneath the petrified shriek. He lashed out at certain death and connected with a solid strike. The high-pitched squeal that followed was all that kept him from running for his life. Professor

Markinson stopped long enough to let his mind process the scene. The two-headed monster was, in fact, two separate bodies. Now, in the glow of the light, he recognized Ahmed holding up Alex, who was steadily rubbing at his jaw.

"You hit me," Alex declared.

"Serves you right for not grabbing my hand," the professor shot back.

"I am not your child," Alex said, stomping forward.

The professor put his hands up in defense. He was far from a natural fighter, and the punch he landed might have been the first of his life.

"This is all your fault," Alex continued. "You've brought me to my death." He seized a handful of the professor's jacket before he could get away. "You've killed us all, you—"

The professor shoved his assistant away with enough force to knock him down. Alex sat on the ground, rubbing his jaw and shaking his head as if disgusted with the right hook more than the abominable creature hunting them in the dark. Ahmed bent over, resting his hands on his knees as he tried to fill his lungs with air. Professor Markinson matched the guide's stance, and the two of them stared at one another, each waiting for the other to speak.

"What happened?" the professor finally asked. "I thought that thing had you."

Ahmed shook his head. "I let you go a moment before it reached me." He stood up straight and revealed the back of his arm. Slashes in his sleeve showed through to bloody cuts underneath. "Not as quick as I should be anymore." He moved the remnants of his sleeve around with his finger and grimaced. "Next time, I might not be so lucky."

"Well, there won't be a next time for me," Alex interjected. He eyed the main path and then headed for it before he continued. "I...I'm not...I'm not saving anyone," he professed. "I am going to climb up to that ledge and get out of here, and if you want to go off in search of Emre and Lauren," he stopped and spun around to face the professor and Ahmed, who had not moved since he started his parting speech, "then you're going to have to do it without me—"

A deafening howl cut the last of his rant short. It came from the shadows of the hall directly behind Alex. Golden eyes pulled free from the darkness, hovering over Alex as the total weight of the beast bore down on him. The body of the thing came down with such ferocity that no one had time to utter a single word before the enormous, gaping mouth was over the top of him.

Professor Markinson saw Ahmed start to run out of the corner of his eye, but he could not move. The professor heard a pitiful, muffled scream before the creature's mouth closed. A single bite cut through Alex at the waist, slicing through his midsection with ease. The creature's head rose as its entire serpentine mass heaved and bobbed, leaving the bloody stump of Alex's remains standing perfectly still.

Ahmed grabbed the professor and forced him to move. The professor wrenched his eyes from the monster as it lunged forward and slurped up the remains of his former assistant. A renewed crunching sound filled the fleeing pair's ears as they dove into a narrow side passage. The walls rose around them, higher than either of them could see over.

Professor Markinson lost sight of the pyramid, but its alluring glow highlighted the darkness on one side of the cavern. He did not have to ask to know for certain precisely where Ahmed was heading. The vision of Alex's brutal death had burned itself into the professor's quickly maddening mind. The raw scene flickered behind his eyes every time he closed them. The crunching sound of the creature gnawing on Alex's bones replaced the thunder of his heart. The professor could not determine if the echo was a product of the beast chasing after them or a permanent terror imprinted on his mind.

Ahmed ran wild, and the distance between him and the professor increased with every step. The sprint pushed Professor Markinson beyond his strength. It was not long before adrenaline and fear were the only things keeping him moving. He rounded a turn and stepped out in the open before he realized it. Ahmed was on his knees, gasping for breath. The dark-skinned man pointed out the way ahead, and the professor took in their surroundings as he slumped back onto the ground.

A new sound engulfed Professor Markinson as he ran his eyes along an expansive waterway coursing from his left to right as far as he could see. Surging water churned within the deep canal, sending splashes over the edge and onto the rear wall of the maze. It took him a moment to realize Ahmed was pointing out something farther away. The expansion ran across the canal, connecting the maze side to a broader road lined with the detestable structures, which filled out the majority of Morgainok.

"A bridge?" Professor Markinson guessed, and Ahmed nodded. They looked over the outline of the city and settled on the mighty pyramid now closer than ever before. He wiped his hand across his face, and the brief break in concentration brought with it the horror of Alex's demise. "He's dead," he whispered.

Ahmed nodded but did not offer any words of condolence. He heaved in a breath and then got back to his feet. "We can still save the others," he said.

The notion nearly caused Professor Markinson to laugh. "You cannot be serious?"

Ahmed's breathing slowed. He looked from the professor to the pyramid. The guide let out one long breath and slid his badly weathered hands to his hips. The blood from his arm dripped from his elbow. He shook his head slowly as he spoke.

"I will not leave Emre to die in this place."

Professor Markinson wanted to yell at the man. He wanted to tell him that the boy was most likely dead, but one look at the determination in his eyes told him it would not matter. Nothing but his own death would stop him in his search. The professor gave in with a heavy sigh. He also knew more than ever that his survival would depend on Ahmed's protection.

A familiar snarl rose over the walls of the maze and spurred the duo to move. Ahmed made directly for the bridge with the professor close behind. Professor Markinson was determined to convince the man to refocus their efforts on a plan of escape, but a sudden shriek from somewhere on the other side of the bridge stopped him. Ahmed stopped mid-step, his head rising higher.

"Lauren," he whispered.

Professor Markinson slowly shook his head as if it could not be, but something told him that it was undoubtedly Lauren. They started again, this time with renewed vigor in their steps. The professor knew the possibility of Emre being with Lauren would drive Ahmed, but his motivations were much more straightforward. If they were able to find one or both of the two remaining members of their expedition, there would be nothing in the way of focusing all their efforts on escape.

10

Lauren blinked in and out. An intense version of the pale glow throughout Morgainok replaced the darkness. The light cut between her eyelids as she wrestled with consciousness. Flashes of memory sparked to life, and a vision of the crowd standing over her forced her eyes apart with sudden panic.

There was no sign of the seemingly endless dark hanging over the city. Lauren stared up at a smoothly cut stone running the length of a small room. Her eyes adjusted quickly to the light in the rock, and she took in her surroundings. The stone walls were barren, the entire chamber void of anything else.

Lauren became aware of her situation all at once. She felt the binds around her wrists, holding her hands together. A pain in her face came from something tied firmly around her head, covering her mouth. She was not sure she could move if she wanted to.

A constant throbbing radiated throughout her head, one she figured had something to do with her unconsciousness. Lauren was playing a mental game with herself, and she knew it. She had played the same game numerous times throughout her life, but she doubted any previous events were ever as life-threatening. The game was simple: Lauren pretended not to be horrified that she was about to surely die and focused her attention on how she would get out of the current predicament. The heinous occurrences of their expedition made the game nearly impossible.

She allowed herself a deep breath, and as she blew it out, Lauren became aware of a sound in the background. The loathsome drumming was absent, replaced by a new subtle hum. It took her a moment to realize the sound was coming from the single opening in the wall directly across from her feet. Lauren identified the sound as a chorus of voices, and the thought produced sizable trepidation.

Lauren rolled to the side and swiftly discovered that the pain radiating from the back of her head was far from her only malady. She was up on her knees when a stinging twinge in her arm matched the thumping in her head. The blood-soaked material around her elbow gave a hint at the problem, but she could not guess what her captors did to her during her abduction. Lauren tried to ignore the pain as she rocked forward and then back, pushing herself up onto her feet. She swayed as her vision blurred but managed to keep herself upright.

Her sense of accomplishment was short-lived. Lauren turned around and discovered she was no longer alone. The face looking back at her was not what she expected. Half her size, the boy stared at her with genuine curiosity. The dark skin of his people framed his slight features, but the ferocity was missing. A single length of cloth hung from his waist, leaving the rest of his feeble physique exposed.

The boy did not move save for tilting his head as he examined her. A fear she did not rightly understand held Lauren still. The boy's apparent innocence was more frightening than the savagery of the mob. She found the source of her apprehension in his eyes.

He gazed back at her in wide-eyed wonder. One eye hinted at a distinct hazel-green, but the other was a repulsive milky white, void of an iris. Lauren grunted at him, attempting a plea for help. The boy did not move. She offered up her bound wrists as an example of her needs. The boy did not move.

Lauren took a step forward, and the curious expression on the boy's face contorted into a disapproving glare. He took a single step backward, and a flurry of commotion erupted from the dark edges of the hall behind him. Men filed into the room in a hurry, quickly surrounding Lauren. They were nearly indistinguishable from one another, each man as scantily covered as the boy was.

Lauren did not have time to consider her options. She was powerless to resist, and her abductors proved it. They came for her all at once, swiftly picking her up off the ground. A chant rang out from them as they lifted her over their heads. She screamed despite her attempt to hold on to her courage, frantically thrashing her arms.

The formation stepped out into the hall and continued on its way, never minding Lauren's hysterical flailing. The passage met its end at an ascending ramp. A sudden intensity of light struck Lauren. The shock of moving out of the confined space brought her wailing to a close. The moment she quieted herself, the full impact of the growing chant overtook her senses.

They were all chanting, her carriers and a multitude of others. The formation rose out into the open and came to a stop. Lauren was reintroduced to the immense darkness above the city of Morgainok. There was no sign of the towering structures, no hint at the cavern walls the expedition team used to climb down into the city. Lauren understood where she was a moment before her carriers lowered her to the ground.

Lying face down on the highest point of the mighty pyramid, she felt the air cool as the men stepped away from her. The intensity of light came from towering bonfires lining the corners of the platform. Lauren locked eyes with Emre. The boy stood lashed to a stake at the edge of the platform, his mouth covered, his legs bound to a pole behind him.

Emre yelled something, but his muffled plea was unrecognizable. Lauren shook as hands grabbed her from behind. She was shocked when someone cut the binds from her wrists. Fear kept her face down, and only after she convinced herself that the knife was not going to be plunged into her back did she consider what to do. Emre's muffled cries never slowed, but Lauren did not respond. Whatever the boy witnessed, it could not save them now.

Lauren slowly slid her hands close to her shoulders and pushed herself up to her knees. The men who carried her stood like statues, lined up along two of the platform's edges. Each man stared at her, watching her every move. Lauren pulled down the piece of cloth tied around her mouth.

She was not sure if she was allowed to move. Lauren was not sure if she should simply jump off the edge of the platform and end her life before they did something horribly unimaginable to her. The sound of a single drumbeat cut through the terrifying silence. The sudden thump caused Lauren to shudder.

Another long quiet washed over the platform, broken again by a drumbeat. The thumping returned with a continuous pattern. The rhythm picked up in pace as Lauren gathered enough courage to stand up. Her new vantage point opened the view around her.

The scene stole Lauren's breath away. An endless sea of black spires filled the surrounding landscape. The pyramid soared over the surrounding structures like a dark tower of old. The mighty cavern walls were lost in the darkness as if Morgainok was at the center of an endless night.

Lauren ran her eyes along the wicked city streets up to the base of the mighty pyramid. She took a stride toward the edge of the platform, and the view of the massive steps of the structure became apparent. Countless figures lined every inch of the staircase, their dark-skinned bodies glistening in the light of fires dotting the immense edifice. She found the source of the detestable drums among the masses.

Lauren locked on to movement midway down the side of the pyramid. A long trail of men worked their way along the broad steps. Several among the train stood out from the others. The procession reached an angular rise along one edge of the pyramid and started up toward the top. Lauren had no idea what the group intended to do once it reached the top, but something in the continuous rise of the rhythm of the drums suggested they represented the culmination of the event.

Lauren turned away from the view as dread consumed her. She glanced at the men surrounding the platform before heading directly toward Emre. The boy lashed about frantically. No one moved, not even when she yanked the gag away from his face.

"Cut me loose," he roared the moment his mouth was free.

"Please."

Lauren looked over his binds and discovered an unfortunate truth.

"I can't," she said.

The announcement forced his mouth close. The boy was still for the first time, the color draining from his face.

"There is some kind of metal cuff," Lauren explained. The realization that she could not help the boy brought with it incredible grief, something more significant than the hopelessness of their situation. She could barely bring herself to look at him.

"Ms. Lauren," Emre said in a tone far too calm for the terror in his eyes. "Don't leave me here."

She did not know how to tell him that they were both going to die. Lauren did not know how to tell him that there was nothing she could do. The recognition caused her to admit her own coming demise. She leaned forward as the pace of the drums grew faster and kissed the boy on the forehead, and then she forced a smile.

"I will stay with you," she said as condolence. Then she added, "As long as I can."

Lauren turned around, stood beside Emre, and discovered one row of the men lining the platform moved. The line parted at the center and revealed a ramp along the edge. The first face to rise from the ramp was the milky-eyed boy she had encountered in the bowels of the pyramid. His curious nature was missing, replaced with a death-like trance. The boy reached the platform before his followers marched into view.

Red billowing feathers peeked over the edge of the platform. The wearer of an impressive headdress strode onto the dais in time with the rhythmic beating of the drums. He wore a long swath of material around his waist, the ends dragging on the ground at his feet. Bone jewelry decorated his chest, arms, and wrists. The man joined the boy standing in the center of the platform.

The trailing party made their way up the ramp with their heads down; each of them lathered in white, the color smeared over their bodies in some ritual preparation. Men and women numbered among them. They found a space near the milky-eyed boy and came to a stop. None of them ever looked at Lauren or Emre throughout the procession, not one ever lifting their head.

The last of them reached the gathering, and by some silent command, the drums came to a sudden stop. Lauren looked to the man in the headdress, whom she guessed to be a priest among them. She found his returning stare jarring. Lauren slid her hand behind Emre and locked her fingers into his. The boy's grip tightened painfully.

All at once, the faces of each of the painted followers looked up. The silent move produced a whimper from Emre. The priest stepped away from the boy and strode toward the outsiders. He stopped directly in front of them, raised his hand, and extended an emaciated finger into Lauren's face.

The priest smiled, revealing a row of teeth lined with stains of rot. He roared out a call in some abominable language, and the entirety of the tribe responded in kind. The reply was resounding, climbing up from the multitude coating the pyramid from its base to the platform. The priest broke into a tirade of vile speech, never taking his bulging eyes off Lauren, never once dropping his hand from her face.

Lauren was too terrified to move. She had to remind herself to breathe once the rant finally ended. The priest took a step back, and the milky-eyed boy took his place. The boy paid little attention to Lauren or Emre, dropping down onto his knees and moving his hand up to his face in some semblance of prayer. The moment his head bowed, the entirety of the painted mass atop the platform moved.

The drumbeat returned with a ferocious tempo. The men lining the edge of the platform descended the ramp in an orderly fashion with the priest trailing the line. The painted throng danced about in place, most of them throwing their hands up over their heads as they howled at the darkness above them. The vision of the madness pressed down on Lauren with enough dread to crush her will.

"It's happening," she said, not positive exactly what *it* was. "God help us."

Emre's lips brushed up against her ear, and his plea faltered under the sound of the chaos. "Save yourself."

The request was enough to pull Lauren toward him. Emre's eyes were sunken, lines of tears streaming down his face.

"Save yourself," he repeated.

Lauren shook her head slowly, unable to take her eyes off his agony. "There's nothing I can do."

Emre swallowed hard. "Reach in my pocket."

Lauren's brow furrowed. She slid her hand down the side of the boy's cargo pants, never taking her eyes off his. She felt the hard exterior of something pressed against his outer thigh. Lauren slipped her hand inside the pocket and ran her fingertips over something cool and metallic.

"You dropped it when they grabbed you," Emre said. "I fell right on top of it when they attacked me."

Words of amazement popped out of her mouth. "My gun." An abrupt silence followed the proclamation. The quiet was so sudden and profound that Lauren had to fight the urge to spin around and fire into the crowd.

The entire gathering stood still, every one of them staring up above at the perfect darkness overhead. A sense of terror gripped Lauren's chest like a vice. She forced her gaze skyward with horrid anticipation. The stillness was complete as nothing dared to move. A collective horror cascaded over the pyramid in a single wave. Something was moving in the dark.

The united apprehension was finally met with a response. A blaring call rang out of the darkness with such power that Lauren was physically moved. The resounding bass was unlike anything she had ever felt. The coming arrival sent the throng atop the platform into a terrifying collective tirade. Lauren pulled out the gun to no effect. The painted faces refused to take their gaze from the sky. The sense of dread heightened by the second until Lauren's limbs shook so badly she could hardly remain standing.

The godly thing pulled away from the darkness in a slow pass. Colossal beyond words and imagination, the wicked being was beyond all measure. An enormous central mass hung in the air, seeping an unctuous film in vast swaths onto the streets of Morgainok. A half dozen limbs dangled beneath the central mass, each the span of an ancient redwood.

It stirred tersely, wrenching the full visage out of the shadows. Lauren's mind nearly broke as she took in the view. A cavernous orifice filled with slithering tentacles expanded, releasing another cry that resonated over the entire city. Its eyeless head bobbed down toward the pyramid as a gargantuan pair of wings worked above the body. The thrust from a single flap pushed the cold air down with tremendous force.

Lauren wrapped her arm around Emre. The painted figures on the platform broke their mindless gaze, each of them searching for an escape. The first few rushed for the descending ramp only to receive several jabs from the tribesmen lining the walkway on the next level down. Many of the painted ones appeared content to die by the spear than await what was to come.

Lauren clung to Emre, and the boy buried his face in her shoulder. The vile drums began their rhythmic pounding as the beast descended from the sky. The pulsating tones drowned out the screams of the painted ones trapped on the platform. A solitary chant arose from the countless natives surrounding the pyramid. The single word was clear above everything else.

NasNoroth.

11

Professor Markinson could not move. The sight of the leviathan was too far beyond his imagination. He trembled with a fear so great he knew his heart would surely stop beating. The scene was far enough away to keep his mind functioning, but barely. A collection of chanting voices brought him back to the moment.

NasNoroth.

A whispered replica slipped from Ahmed's mouth. "NasNoroth."

The professor stumbled as the world sped up around him. His mind was moving at a blistering pace, and he could not slow it down enough to make sense of anything. Neither of the two men could pull their eyes away from the darkness above the pyramid and the godlike creature hovering there. The beast boomed a horrendous call, and the shock from the wave forced the professor back another step.

"We have to go back," Professor Markinson heard himself say.

The muscles in Ahmed's face tensed at the sound of the declaration. His apprehension was evident in every detail, but he still could not look away from the thing he had called NasNoroth.

"This is what you wanted to see, yes?"

The professor slowly shook his head, still fighting the terror driving him to run away. "Not like this," he muttered. "Nothing like this."

"They're sacrificing to the god," Ahmed said. "They're making an offering."

Professor Markinson did not grasp the implication at first. "I don't —"

"Emre is there, on the top," he said, pointing at the highest level of the pyramid.

"You don't know that," Professor Markinson shot back. "There's no way you could know that."

Ahmed looked away from the monstrosity overhead for the first time since it appeared. The whites of his eyes stood out prominently within the shadows of their hidden position. "We have to try," Ahmed insisted.

His words took a moment to process. It hit the professor all at once, and he roared back much louder than he intended. "You're mad." He grabbed Ahmed by the arms. "That boy is dead." The harshness of his words was beyond him, and he regretted saying it the moment he realized what he had done. His regret had little to do with the boy's safety and more to do with his ability to influence his guide.

Ahmed easily wrenched himself away from the professor and took a step back. The two men's eyes never left one another. Ahmed's stance shifted, raising his arms out in front, prepared to defend himself if necessary. Professor Markinson had a sudden recognition of his shortcomings. It was plain to him that he could not survive on his own. Alex's death left him with few options.

"This is suicide," the professor said, softening his stance as well as his tone. "We shouldn't needlessly throw our lives away." Ahmed remained tense. "Alex is gone; we know that. You and I have seen for ourselves the terrors that lurk here." He pointed up at the monstrous creature hovering in the distance. "How could we hope to survive such a thing?"

Professor Markinson could barely contain his terror. The adrenaline of the moment was passing with every breath, leaving the sheer dread of their situation to take its place. He did not dare to look up at the leviathan. He continued to deny that it was even there in order to keep control.

Ahmed stared him down with little response to his reasoning. The big man finally gave a deep sigh as he took in a breath. He put his hands on his hips and pursed his lips. His response, however, was not what the professor hoped.

"I must know."

Professor Markinson fought the urge to snap back at him. Ahmed held his hand up before the professor could get anything else out.

"Up there," he said, and the professor followed his finger toward something behind them. "It's our best hope."

The edge of the cavern was barely visible. A narrow patch of open ground ran along the edge of the canal beyond the outer wall of the ghastly maze, at its northernmost end. Professor Markinson could not make out the details within the shadows, but he ran his eyes along the cavern wall up to a ledge high up on the rocky face. The vision instantly produced a recall.

"The outcropping," he mused as the memory of Alex, Ahmed, and his conversation popped into his head. "We could find another set of tunnels." The professor had nearly forgotten the find altogether. "That is it," he said with renewed hope. "Let's go now." He started forward and came to a jarring halt when Ahmed grabbed his collar. "What the hell?"

Professor Markinson spun around as Ahmed took a long step forward. The two men came together a nose apart.

"I will help you, but I will not leave until we work our way along the edge of the cliff, and I can see the pyramid for myself," Ahmed explained directly. "There is no other way," he added before the professor could object.

The professor began a calculation of sorts. He quickly worked through several possibilities, each with a hasty probability factor assigned to it. No matter how he tried, the professor could not give himself any real chance of survival going it on his own. He ground his teeth before spitting out the foul-tasting word.

"Agreed."

Ahmed led them away from the bridge, following along the lip of the canal. There was no need for conversation. The professor had little to offer, and Ahmed was in no mood for the interruption.

They worked their way around the far edge of the maze, heads moving between the colossal creature in the distance and the shadowy path before them. A quick jog covered the distance to the lower land between the cavern wall and the canal. The shimmer of water brought them to a stop.

"What now?" Professor Markinson asked.

The way ahead revealed itself when they stepped down into the shadows concealing the cavern floor from afar. Murky water covered the ground dotted with flat stones resting several yards apart. The shimmering surface reached the cavern wall on one side and ran the entire length back to the canal in the other direction and all the way to the base of the pyramid ahead of them.

"We'll have to use the stepping stones to cross," Ahmed surmised.

His follow-up died in his throat as a thunderous wail echoed across the darkness, saturating the entire monstrous cavern in a wall of horrific sound. The professor forced himself to turn toward the leviathan and take in the whole sight of the foul god. The enormous mass swept downward with a flap of its glistening wings. The move exposed several reedy appendages reaching up from the hunched spine of the beast into the darkness overhead. The vast web of limbs gave a sudden explanation for how the thing held up its vast girth beyond the strength of its meager wings. The professor scarcely had time to process the information before Ahmed's actions compelled him to move.

"Wait for me."

Ahmed trod lightly, jumping forward the moment his boot touched the center of the stepping stones. The guide was several stones away before the professor gathered up the courage to spring from the edge of the water. He had fleeting thoughts about how they would climb the rock face, but there was no time to reconsider. He reached the first stepping stone and froze, his momentum nearly spilling him over into the water.

The professor steadied himself, and once he was sure he was not about to take a dip, he looked up at the pyramid. The leviathan's descent was met was a shrilling cry of hundreds of voices. A rise in the heathenistic drums matched the chorus as the beat picked up. The great elder creature opened the pit at the center of its head, and a mass of unctuous tentacles slithered out from within.

 The sudden burst of noise spurred the professor on. He sprang forward and hit his mark, this time continuing to keep his momentum going. Professor Markinson attempted to block out the rising fear growing with every beat of the damnable drums. He lost count of his jumps before he realized Ahmed was no longer in front of him.

"Ahmed," he said, attempting to whisper and yell at the same time. The rising echo of screams among the backdrop of the drums made it impossible to hear anything. "Ahmed," he repeated, rising to an official shout.

Professor Markinson ran his eyes from the stone directly ahead of him, across the surface of the water, up to the side of the cavern. The first hint of movement came from a single bubble breaking the water's surface, not two stepping stones in front of him. He leaped ahead and stopped as something glistened beneath the water.

He leaned forward, and the shimmering effect produced movement beyond him. His sudden awareness revealed multiple disturbances beneath the surface. The effect grew all around him until the water churned in every direction. The professor bent over, close enough to reach out and touch the surface of the water, although he would not dare. A swift flash of movement produced a clear view of something beneath.

There was a mix of scales, oddly blue-green; however, a hint of some fleshy skin caused him to pull back with involuntary revulsion. The water continued to churn until filling the space between the stepping stones. The shimmering scales broke the surface all around him. Professor Markinson stood unmoving, paralyzed by his fear. His mind begged him to turn back, but he could not will himself to move.

An explosion near the lip of the canal broke the professor's internal deliberation. Ahmed flung himself upward and out of the water before slamming his back down onto a stone. Something had hold of him. They were the size of the big man's head, each of them covered in glistening scales. Fleshy nubs latched onto his dark, exposed skin, more of them than the professor could count.

Professor Markinson did not move, not even when Ahmed cried out for him. One of the scaly mounds clung to the side of his face. Ahmed grabbed hold of it and yanked it away. The thing came off with a line of Ahmed's skin clinging to a pulsing gap in the center of its body. Blood ran down the man's face, and he kicked and screamed. He pulled at them one at a time, each of them taking a chunk of his flesh as they were pried away.

Ahmed slipped as he got to his feet. Blood covered the remains of his clothes. He heaved in gulps of air as he tried to steady himself. The professor reached him quickly in a haze after an adrenaline-fueled dance across the stepping stones. Ahmed was down on one knee, blood running down his arm and over the gun in his hand.

"You still have your gun," the professor said.

Ahmed did not respond, only nodding and raising the weapon up by his head.

Professor Markinson jumped again, landing a single stepping stone away from him. "You are hurt badly," he said without much thought. "You won't make that climb." The professor got a better look at the man, and the gouges in his clothes showed through to open sections of exposed tissue beneath. "I can still make it," he said, barely audible.

Ahmed's eyes slid up to meet Professor Markinson's gaze. The professor knew what he meant to do without ever admitting it to himself. Self-preservation would rule the day, and he meant to give himself the best possible chance of survival. He saw that chance resting in the wounded big man's grip.

Ahmed placed his free hand over a wound on his chest and re-adjusted his hold on his gun. "You never meant to help the others."

Professor Markinson did not have to respond. He knew the statement was true without having to say it aloud. Somewhere deep down, he knew he would never have helped Ahmed find Emre and Lauren once they got up on the ledge. What he did not know was what he was going to do about it now.

The churning water all around them hinted at what was to come. The shimmering scaly hides of the pod creatures broke the surface near Ahmed. Their fleshy truncated appendages stretched toward the flat rock and took hold. Professor Markinson sent a hard kick into the side of one, reaching up for his foot.

The professor's retort cut straight to the point. "Give me the gun."

Ahmed's labored breathing intensified by the second. His brow furrowed between his eyes as he stared down the professor. There was no way to tell how many rounds remained in the gun; however, Professor Markinson was willing to wager that a single bullet could mean the difference between survival and horrendous death. Both men were forced to take their eyes off one another to stave off the vile creatures swarming up around their respective stepping stones.

"You will not make it out of here alive," Ahmed assured him. "Your dark fascination will be the death of us all." He swayed backward toward the edge of the canal, catching himself at the last moment.

"You're dying," Professor Markinson announced, feeling emboldened by the bigger man's increasing weakness. He repeated his demand. "Give me the gun." He extended his hand, glancing at the distance between them. The roaring elation atop the pyramid came to a crescendo as the elder god's appendages darted from its gaping maw down into a herd of figures on the precipice. Professor Markinson felt one of the pod creatures latch onto his boot, and he knew the time for debate had passed. "Give it to me, now."

He did not give Ahmed time to respond. The professor leaped

forward, striking Ahmed in the chest with the high point of his shoulder. They tumbled backward as the professor grabbed hold of the gun with both hands. The two men hit the water intertwined, each struggling for control of the weapon.

The darkness devoured them in an instant. Shock temporarily froze the professor as the freezing water consumed him. A singe of pain ran up his leg as something bit into his calf. Another sting struck his forearm. He instinctually let go of the gun, grabbing onto the slimy thing clamping onto him. The professor managed to tear one of the creatures away from his arm, but not before another latched onto his back.

He burst from the water in agonizing pain. He glimpsed Ahmed pulling himself up onto the lip of the canal and swam toward him, ignoring the swelling heat in his legs. Ahmed caught his eyes and shook his head. He heaved in a deep breath and offered one last decree.

"You will burn in hell."

The professor launched forward but could not cover the distance before Ahmed dropped over the side of the canal, taking the gun with him. The professor propelled himself again, this time slamming into the edge of the rocky lip of the canal at his chest. He tugged frantically at the fiend chomping on his back and flung the thing away as two more bumped up against his legs beneath the water. Professor Markinson stared out at the swift churning flow within the canal. There was no sign of Ahmed.

The roaring mob surrounding the mighty pyramid erupted again, but the professor did not dare to peer at their abhorrent god. He kicked the lone scaly beast off his leg and screamed as it took a piece of him with it. Professor Markinson spun his legs around and dangled them over the edge of the canal. In one final attempt to save himself, he pushed off and dropped down into the black current below.

12

No words could soothe Lauren's petrified mind. Nothing on earth prepared her to look upon the elder thing. It hung in the dark cavernous sky, glistening, leathery wings flapping out beside the gargantuan mass. A web of broad limbs spread out above the body, spanning beyond sight. A gaping orifice opened at the peak of its eyeless head, a tangled mess of oozing feelers darting into the air.

Every muscle in Lauren's body tensed at once as she struggled for control. The painted faces of those pour souls chosen for the offering pressed in on one another. Their palpable fear spoke to the knowledge of the coming event. Lauren would not guess it until the feast began.

A wide splatter of secretion struck the crowd as the leviathan's feelers sprang forth—a pair of tentacles wrapped around a painted woman and yanked her off the ground in an instant. The elder thing took hold of a man as the woman disappeared into its awaiting cavity. The painted-faced offerings broke in ranks, fleeing their destiny with wild panic. The rush from the pack spurred Lauren to move.

"We have to get you free," she stammered as she turned her attention on the bindings holding Emre to the pole. She put the gun in her pocket and went to work on the knot.

"It is no use," the boy replied, yelling in the face of the elder creature. "Save yourself."

Lauren slid her finger through the ties, producing a glimmer of hope. The prospect came to a terrifying end as Emre's entire body lifted straight up.

"Emre."

Lauren's eyes shot up to find the boy already midair, most of his body intertwined between several of the slithering feelers. She darted toward the roaring bonfire at the nearest corner of the platform and reached in for one of the burning logs without a thought for her bare hand. The pain bit her quickly once she grabbed hold. Lauren spun around and flung the red-hot ember at the elder thing. The flame struck the tangle of feelers wrapped around Emre, burning through the layer of mucus on contact.

The response was instant but not what Lauren had hoped. At least a dozen more tentacles slashed down from the beast's mouth. Several slipped into the scurrying crowd, snatching bodies up with sudden spasms. A pair of appendages slipped around Lauren's waist before she could get out of the way. The compression came quickly, pulling in against her sides until her ribs nearly cracked.

She was in the air, rising toward the pulsating mouth, unable to scream. Her entire body spun as the view of the pyramid slipped out from under her. There was nothing beyond the leviathan and the endless darkness within its throbbing cavity. Clouds of white filled her eyes as the last of the air gushed from her lungs.

Lauren's hands dropped over the squeezing tentacles as her head fell back and the tips of her fingers slid over the gun in her pocket. She clung to the last fragment of consciousness, beseeching her hand to pull the weapon free. The actions that followed were beyond her awareness as she moved without calculated thought. She pressed the barrel of the gun against the oozing surface of the limb wrapped around her and pulled the trigger.

An internal will to survive urged Lauren's lungs to gulp in the air when the pressure around her body released. The sensation of falling came from the feeling of her gut rising into her throat. Lauren's eyes opened, and the clouds dissipated in time to watch Emre's lifeless body slurped into the leviathan's awaiting cavity. The horrendous sounds of Morgainok flooded through the haze in her mind a split second before she made contact.

Lauren hit the sloping side of the pyramid feet first. The shocking impact sent an unspeakable jolt up her spine and into the base of her skull. She tumbled head over feet beyond her control. The edge of consciousness slinked through her thoughts as Lauren slid to a halt.

Fear was the only thing capable of driving her to move. She sat up, trying to take in her surroundings. The first thing she realized was that she was alone. There was no sign of the tribespeople she was sure would be there to drag her back to the mass sacrifice. She could hear them all at once, the dreadful wailing song of the natives backed by the never-ending beating of the drums.

Lauren's vision cleared as she forced herself to stand. She looked back and found herself several stories down the north face of the pyramid. The gargantuan elder thing continued its feast; more than a dozen of the painted-faced offerings dangled within the hideous mess of its feelers. She stood on one of the flat surfaces of the pyramid, midway between the summit platform and the expansive surrounding roadway at its base.

She ran. There was no other thought to process. Lauren's instinct to survive had complete control. She lost her gun in the fall and knew there was nothing else to save her but her sheer will to endure.

The rhythm of the drums altered sharply as if to match the escapee's every step. They were coming for her, rows of the dark-skinned souls racing toward Lauren from the higher platforms. Several of them waved spears in the air above their heads, shouting blasphemies at her in their vile speech. Lauren ran frantically toward a descending ramp at the far end of the path and bolted downward three steps at a time.

She did not realize she was yelling until her throat burned from the act. Her foot hit the flat surface of the ensuing path, but her momentum would not allow her to change course. Lauren rushed over the edge with wild abandonment and started down the sloped face of the pyramid. She nearly lost her footing several times but somehow managed to stay upright.

Lauren neared the wide road surrounding the pyramid's base when she discovered a group of tribespeople rushing toward her.

They cleared the first row of the dark structures surrounding the pyramid from an adjoining road. Lauren never slowed; instead, forcing herself to run faster, she stepped onto solid flat ground and then raced across the road and in between the buildings. The darkness of Morgainok quickly swallowed her as she searched for a place to hide.

Lauren turned to the right and then back to the left after several long strides. She crossed two side passages before she slowed. The structures rose up around her quickly, leaving only a view of the pyramid's highest point and the dark god hovering over it. The edifices muffled the chaotic sounds of the drums along with the depraved shrieks of the natives.

She managed to soften the thundering beats of her heart. The resumption of control helped to highlight several crucial noises. The slapping steps of her pursuers were some distance away. Lauren had apparently lost them in her maddening race. There was another echoing between the structures, and she knew it well.

The canal.

Lauren slid to a stop and pressed her back against the wall of a tower. The black structure rose high above her, its shadow consuming her completely. The faint light in the rock produced a familiar glow about her. The respite allowed Lauren to gather her nerve and catch her breath, but it also allowed her mind to come to terms with the effects of her fall.

Something warm ran down her brow and onto her cheek. She wiped her hand over her face and pulled back a crimson-covered palm. Somehow seeing the blood made the pain increase tenfold. Her knees burned from the inside, adding to a throbbing shock in her hip. Lauren nearly collapsed as the adrenaline waned and the ache sunk in. She wondered if she could get her legs to move again if she had to.

Lauren held on to the hope that if she could reach the chilling waters of the canal, she could get away. There was no connection between the thought and any real plan of escape, but she was in desperate need of a goal. The canal was something she could aim for, something to target. Her mind could not process anything else.

Lauren bent over at the waist and pressed her hands on her knees. She watched the blood drip from above her eye and pool on the cavern floor. The slapping sounds of her pursuers drew closer, and she knew she could not wait any longer. Lauren sprang into motion, swallowing the excruciating ache running up and down her spine.

The way between the towering structures narrowed, forcing her to turn off into a roadway. Lauren was confident someone or something was going to reach out from the dark recesses at every turn. The awful sounds of the sacrifice and the chorus of screams lessened with every step as the churning of the water grew louder. The maddening drums continued, resonating between the structures as if the very instruments were on the hunt.

Lauren remained on the roadway and was soon rewarded for her effort. The edge of the canal came quickly as the road deadened directly ahead. Waves splashed over the side in regular intervals, leaving the edge of the road covered in thin pools. Her pace slowed as she approached, and her heart seized in her chest when a whispered voice called out to her by name from the darkness.

Lauren knew she should run. She knew any hesitation could bring about her demise. A hand reached out of the shadows, and the owner's face crept forward. Lauren managed to keep a shrill buried in her throat.

His eyes locked onto hers as the man stepped into the glow of the pale light. He looked like death. His frailty hid the strength Lauren had come to associate with him. It took her a moment to get his name out in the open.

"Ahmed?" The word was almost foreign to her. She was sure she would never see any of her group again. "Ahmed," she repeated with more confidence.

The emotions sprang from some buried place in her heart she had hidden away. Lauren was so sure she would never see a familiar face again that the appearance was overwhelming. She leaped forward, wrapping her arms around the big man's neck. It was not until he nearly fell over that she realized something was terribly wrong.

"I found it," he stammered as she let go of him and backed away.

Lauren got a clear view of Ahmed and discovered the stains of blood along his side and a hint at more damage to one of his legs. He pressed his hand against the closest structure lining the road and leaned over. Lauren thought he might fall if not for the support. He took a deep breath and looked up at her.

"What happened?" she whispered.

Ahmed slowly shook his head as he took another long breath. "There's no time," he said. "There's a bridge over the canal not far from here." He motioned his head in the direction of the narrow path behind him. "It leads to some kind of storage area." He had to stop. Lauren kept quiet as Ahmed's chest swelled and then relaxed, and he was able to continue. "There's grain and corn." He clenched his jaw. "They must get it from somewhere above ground. There's a steep pathway leading up the backside of the canyon wall." His eyes opened wide. "That must be the way out."

Lauren nodded, having no idea how she was going to live long enough to use the information. Ahmed convulsed, and Lauren instinctively grabbed him. She felt the full weight of the big man as his hand slipped off the side of the building. Lauren eased him toward her and helped him lie down on the cool canyon floor.

Ahmed kept his eyes on her as he convulsed again. Blood sprayed from his mouth as he coughed, leaving a line of scarlet running down from the corner of his mouth. He pushed his hand under his belt and pulled out his gun. Ahmed pressed the weapon against her.

"Take it," he said.

Lauren hesitated before she gathered the courage to tell him what she figured he wanted to know. "Emre…he didn't—" She stopped as his grip tightened around her wrist.

"Someone has to make it out," he said, refusing to hear anymore. "You can do this."

Lauren did not think she would survive another hour, let alone long enough to escape.

Ahmed's grip tightened more. "You have to stay alive."

Lauren was struggling with what she should say to the dying man. She thought to tell him everything would be okay because that was what people did in desperate times. The problem was that Lauren had never been very good at saying what everyone expected her to. This moment was no different. She quickly found herself and remained faithful to her heart.

"We're both going to die down in this awful place, darling," she said and forced a grin. She felt an odd sense of satisfaction in the smile that formed on Ahmed's face. He coughed several times, expanding the line of blood on his face to a wide patch on the ground. A long shadow stretched its way over Ahmed's face, interrupting their moment of escapism. Lauren looked up in time to see a pair of tribesmen rushing toward them. "I hate to say I told you so."

Lauren popped up and raised the gun. Unsure of how many rounds remained, she was prepared to empty the clip. She aimed at the frontrunner of the charging group. A flurry of teeth and eyes cut through the darkness as the men held spears up above their heads. Lauren's finger tensed, but a desperate plea held her in place.

"No."

Ahmed's cracking voice cut through her concentration.

"Run."

The big man grunted as he rolled over and then forced himself to stand.

"Get out of here."

"You can't—"

Lauren staggered as Ahmed pushed her and sprinted away.

"Go now."

Lauren was running before she knew what was happening. Ahmed's war cry carried through the darkness with her, above the drums' thunder and the countless horde's carnal roar. Lauren adjusted her grip on the gun, and the weight of it gave her strength. There was nothing left for her; only the need to survive remained.

The sound of the rushing water chased her as she ran along the edge of the canal. The patter of bare feet hissed in the wind somewhere in the distance. They were coming, she knew, which meant Ahmed was gone. Lauren felt it in her gut, but her deadened emotions kept it from her heart.

The desperation built with each passing moment. Lauren focused on the edge of the canal, determined to reach Ahmed's footbridge. Shadows covered every other step, and the pale blue lines in the rock provided only a hint of what lay ahead. The buildings parted before she realized it, and Lauren found herself standing on a passageway wider than any she had seen before.

A glance over the shoulder revealed the enormous pyramid in all its horrifying glory in the distance. The leviathan was gone, hidden somewhere in the pitch-blackness shrouding the sky over Morgainok. Lauren faced the waterway, seeing for the first time a way across. She ran her eyes over the narrow extension and was stunned to find someone staring back at her from the other side.

13

Professor Markinson hunched over close to the ground, trying to remain as quiet as humanly possible. The two dozen or so figures standing out in the open did not know where he was, but something had alerted them of his closeness. He had nearly drowned. The churning canal water was as black as night, and it was impossible to tell which direction was up once submerged.

He had thrown himself up on the steep embankment with the last of his strength, avoiding death by mere seconds. It took him a long time to gather both the breath and energy to move again. He had crawled up to the edge of the canal and rolled over onto the cold, flat cavern floor. Part of him considered lying there in the dark and waiting for death to catch up with him finally.

Fear got him to his feet again. The professor discovered he was still on the western side of the canal, how far beyond the dreaded maze he did not know. He could see plainly the colossal pyramid across from him. He beheld the leviathan god with dizzying detail and whispered its name for his own dreadful delight.

"NasNoroth."

The horror of it clung to his heart. He doubted he would ever be able to remove the scar of the memory from his mind. The vision was like nothing he had ever imagined. The black books and ancient scrolls did not prepare the mind for such a sight. Against all odds, he had found Ahmed. He followed the rouge guide from the shadows but lost him when he stumbled upon a pack of the natives. The professor was on the run. He had no direction, no hope to escape, and a gnawing hunger sapping every remaining ounce of energy from within.

Professor Markinson set his mind on returning to the cavern wall and climbing up to the elusive ledge. He cursed Ahmed for leaving him on his own. The professor made no excuses for his actions. If Ahmed had simply handed over the gun, the two of them might have still had a chance. *At least I would have*, the professor silently concluded.

Movement from the tribesmen refocused the professor's attention. They split into several smaller groups of two and three. A series of instructions in their foreign grunted speech sent the lesser factions off in every direction at once. Professor Markinson slowly slid down onto his stomach and lay prone. He held his breath as a pair of outlines stepped in his direction.

He could do nothing, not even when the hunters were close enough to hear his breathing. The rising beat of the professor's heart thumped in his ears. He was certain they would hear him. A haze of white pressed in from the corners of his eyes as his brain begged for air. Professor Markinson held on until the burn in his lungs was too much to bear. The exhale was quick and as quiet as possible. He risked a turn of his head and discovered he was all alone in the dark.

The relief was short-lived. A faint sound swept over him as he dared to rise to his knees. The guttural snarl caused the hairs on the back of his neck to rise. A heavy step came next.

There was something there in the dim light, something working its way along the edge of the cavern wall. Professor Markinson hesitantly moved. He scrambled forward, keeping close to the canal. The professor's pace quickened, and the thing in the dark sped up to keep stride.

"It has me," he whimpered.

His mind was torn. The one direction he wanted to go was the only one he dared not seek out. Another snarl closed in, and the professor jutted away from the canal, rushing toward a low set of structures. The cavern floor dropped down sharply, and he found himself struggling to keep from falling over. The professor worked his way down in a low depression before realizing the structures were at the center of a long basin encircling a higher rise in the rock.

Professor Markinson's feet never stopped moving. The snarl of the thing increased in volume, rising to its peak once its prey reached the bottom of the depression. The pale lines embedded in the rock revealed the enormity of the conclave. The sides rose sharply on either side of him, centering on several towers.

A wall bordered the epicenter, and a flutter of movement pierced the darkness as something leaped from the highest tower. It had wings for sure, but the details were lost in the shadows. Professor Markinson slowed to a crawl as the creature circled high above. He felt trapped, like a wild animal hiding from a pack of hungry wolves.

The professor pushed himself to run, convinced the beast overhead was only holding him still long enough, so whatever awful thing was following him could catch up. He turned back toward the incline and the only landmark he knew. The burn in his legs intensified with every step. A swoosh of air greeted him midway up the embankment as the winged creature came in for a closer view.

Professor Markinson got a glimpse of it, but the sight was enough to give it away. It was all eyes and frail feelers. A wide jaw centered under the body with a lengthy pair of wings sprouting at the spine. It let out a dreadful screech as it swept by overhead.

The hellacious call was enough to spur the professor to move faster. He pushed himself until there was nothing left. Filled with a mix of dread and disappointment, Professor Markinson realized once he stopped that he was hardly midway up the immense embankment. He rested his hands on his knees, his chest heaving. The entirety of the basin lay before him, and Professor Markinson made a connection almost immediately.

"For Caesar," he said.

Even among the savages, he guessed, there must be entertainment. The point of it came to him all at once. The central towers could hold quite the crowd; he thought as he ran his eyes along the dark walls. Another creature lifting off the highest peak broke his introspective. The professor did not fully understand the game afoot, but he was quick enough to see he was the prey. The return of the heinous snarl pulled him toward the lowest point of the bowl, where something came trudging out of the darkness.

The distance was too great for particulars, but sections of hardened shell gleamed in the low light. Rows of short, thick legs pushed the beast ahead, gathering speed with every stride. Another snarl escaped from mouths on both sides of its flat head. Professor Markinson made no connection with the thing or any wicked species he kept stored away in his mind. He gave the vision only a split second more before turning to run.

His mind told him that the short legs of the brute could not possibly climb the steep rise. In his mind's eye, he could see the embankment lined with countless rows of tribespeople, shouting in their unholy tongue at some godless spectacle meant to take place in the hollow. The professor was determined not to die playing the game. The top of the bowl was in sight, and he pressed on against every fiber in his body.

He popped up and over the rim and collapsed the moment his boots touched the level ground. The sound of the trampling brute was lost somewhere down in the hollow, but he knew he was far from safe. A distant shrill was quickly answered by another screech from somewhere out in the darkness. A quick scan showed he had covered very little ground in his detour. The cavern wall was farther away than when he started. The professor pushed himself off the ground and took in the view of the glowing pyramid.

The canal was somewhere ahead of him. The professor made a hasty decision to follow the waterway as far as it would go. He hoped that it would lead to some underground depression. If he were lucky, the waterway would end near the elusive ledge on the cavern wall, and he would be able to make his climb.

The professor took two steps but then froze. It was not the ferocious snarl or the stealthy flapping wings from somewhere overhead, nor was it the sound of the drums. The silence reached down into Professor Markinson's soul and held him. He scanned the glow in the darkness, noting every inch of the Morgainok cityscape. The colossal pyramid stood motionless save the towering fires at its peak.

He had to force himself to move. An echo met the first step, followed by another pair of footsteps moving toward him from the left. Professor Markinson sped up, and the move produced a rustling flurry on his right. He was running before he processed what was happening.

They were close, and the first excited shriek cut through the silence like a knife. A swell of sound followed the shout, and a chorus of guttural yells nearly thrust the professor forward. A wall of sound took over as if all of Morgainok had held its breath in anticipation of what was to come. The professor ran with a haze of madness blinding his thoughts.

They yelled and screamed at him, joining in some noxious song. The professor ran wild, his blood pumping through his body at maximum capacity. He had one chance to survive, and as best he could tell, it was directly out in front of him. The canal opened up after several long strides, and the professor dove for it. He was airborne when something bit into his leg, sending a wave of fire up his thigh.

The pain came as he fell, the sounds of the whipping stream within reach. The cold struck like a stone as he sank beneath the surface of the water. He tried to swim, but the moment he kicked his legs, the searing sting robbed him of his strength. The professor had to depend on his arms to keep him from drowning. The action proved difficult, and he swallowed mouthfuls of the drink, trying to stay afloat.

He let the current take him, losing sight and the sound of the hunters along the edge of the canal. The steep wall was close. The professor used his hands to slow himself along the flat rock embankment. Once the moment was right, he pressed on the stone and heaved his body out of the tide. He lay on the incline for an insufferable time, not sure there was a reason for him to move.

The professor knew before he looked that he was shot. Somehow seeing the arrow protruding from his hamstring made the pain nearly unbearable. Amid his internal struggle, he heard a clear yell from somewhere on the opposite side of the canal. The sound yanked him from his gloom; he recognized the words as clearly as his own.

"Go now."

This was not the depraved jargon of one of *them,* nor was it the haunting snarl of one of Morgainok's foul minions. The sting of hope got him to climb the rest of the way up the incline on his stomach. He tore two long swaths from the bottom of his shirt and sat up on his side. He slipped his hand over the end of the arrow's shaft and found the head embedded below the skin.

The professor told himself he had survived worse injuries, although he was unsure if that was true. He pulled the arrow out in one quick motion and nearly bit the tip of his tongue off in an attempt to keep quiet. A hasty operation covered the wound with one section of his makeshift bandages; then, he tied it in place with the other. He was satisfied that there was not a pool of his blood circling him on the ground when he was finished.

It took him several tries to stand, his leg unwilling to support the weight of his body. He managed to walk upright in a grueling step and sway motion. He gathered himself every couple of feet, determined to keep going. The professor followed the canal, keeping it within a few feet. Something broke the open view over the canal up ahead.

Professor Markinson crouched down low, and his body trembled from the pain in his leg. His fear helped him sweep the ache aside. He took a few steps and confirmed that his newly found expansion did cross the canal. His eyes worked over the faint outline of the buildings within the glow of the light in the street.

A swift movement focused him on a single figure rushing through the dark. He crept closer, reaching the opening to the bridge. The figure came to a stop in the roadway on the other side. The slight frame held the professor still. She turned toward him, and the sound of her voice struck him when she called out.

"Professor?"

14

"Professor?" Lauren's head juddered. "Is that you?"

The professor slowly slid a finger up to his lips. His eyes widened as he peered out into the surrounding darkness. A chill ran down Lauren's spine. The fright in his face screamed out to her across the expanse.

The filthy man was very different from the reserved and often pompous professor she remembered. His clothes were dripping wet, the pant legs and shirtsleeves in ribbons. Blood marked one side of his chest and another large blotch on his leg. The bandage around his thigh would have been laughable had it not been for the obvious pain it caused him. He opened his mouth but sat there stooped over in silence as if he had somehow lost the ability to form words.

Lauren walked toward him slowly, half expecting him to howl at any moment. The professor held his stare with a bewildered expression, his finger still up against his lips. Lauren stopped in the center of the bridge, unsure if it was safe to continue. Professor Markinson put his hand down and appeared to come back from some faraway place.

"Lauren."

Her name came in a broken croak, but it was familiar enough for her to make it out. The fear in his eyes forced her to crouch to match his stance. He gazed over his shoulder into the dark and then waved her forward. Lauren came to a stop, a foot from his face.

"What the hell happened to you?" she asked.

It took him several seconds to process the information. "Alex is dead."

The bluntness struck her with solid impact. "Emre too," she said, nearly having to force it out. "Ahmed...he..." she stopped. Her eyes popped open. "He told me how to get out of here."

The professor's gaze found her again, this time with a dogged glare. He leaned in close enough for Lauren to feel his breath on her cheek.

"You saw him?"

Lauren nodded, not positive why she felt a sudden need to lie to the man. She distrusted him for sure, but that stemmed from his blame for leading the group down into the repugnant black city. This new suspicion felt different. Lauren slid her hand over the gun in her pocket and quickly decided to keep the knowledge of it to herself.

"Yes," she said. "Not long ago." She motioned with a nod behind her. "He found what he believed was a way out. Hell, I don't know if it really is or not," she admitted. "But it might be the best chance we have at surviving this."

Professor Markinson took a step back, and his follow-up felt oddly out of place. "What else did he tell you?"

Lauren hesitated. "Nothing," she said, her eyes narrowing. "Why?"

A familiar sound broke the stare-off that followed. The drums picked up a roaring, steady beat. They felt closer than ever before, thumping to the pace of a quick march. Lauren pushed her suspicion aside and thought back to Ahmed's hurried directions.

"We need to continue on from this side of the bridge," she remembered. "There's some kind of storage area for food and supplies at the cavern wall." She did not wait for a response. "Come on."

The professor latched onto her hand as she slipped past him. They ran out into the vast cavern together, carefully avoiding the colosseum of foul games as he described it in hushed tones. The effect of learning that there were flying beasts compelled Lauren to look up into the darkness every couple of strides. The distance was far greater than she expected from Ahmed's hasty directions, but the destination was evident. It was impossible to tell by the continuing beat of the drums if they were being followed, but there was no doubt about what lay ahead. The movement was clear and easy to monitor. Professor Markinson yanked on Lauren's arm and brought them to a stop.

The cavern's colossal wall stretched up high into the dark. The soft streaks of light highlighted the elusive cliff pass several stories up the face. Lauren found the seed of Ahmed's plan in a narrowly twisted fissure in the wall leading from the floor up to the high pass. The hidden entrance to the fissure lay behind a series of dark structures erected in a semicircle adjacent to the cavern wall. Several shadowy figures moved through an intense light within the semicircle of structures.

"That's it," Lauren announced unceremoniously. "That's how we get out."

Professor Markinson shook his head. "If we go in there, we'll be trapped." He looked back the way they came. "There has to be another way."

Lauren wrenched her hand away from him. "If you want to go traipsing back out into the city, be my guest." She started forward. "I'm going to take Ahmed's suggestion and get the hell out of here."

Professor Markinson tried to get another point in, but Lauren was too far away from him to hear his whispers. He had to run to catch up with her. He fell in step as they neared the exterior side of the structures. The echoes wafting through the lone point of entry caused Lauren's heart to skip a beat.

It was a gnarling growl, deep and menacing. Nothing could equal the soul-shaking horror that NasNoroth produced, but something in that sound came close. Lauren pressed her back against the structure's exterior closest to the semicircle opening and waited until the professor was next to her. They edged along the construction until a sliver of the interior came into view.

Wide-open archways lined the cavern walls along the interior side of the buildings. Several tribespeople, primarily women, were steady at work. They stood in line holding baskets on their heads. Someone inside the structures filled the containers, and then the carrier would move on, out of sight.

Lauren leaned out as far as she could to get a look without stepping into the open. The basket carriers formed another line at the base of the fissure in the cavern wall. One by one, they started up, climbing on crude stairs only partially visible from Lauren's viewpoint. The sweat built on her brow as the reality of their impossible plan bore down on her.

Lauren twisted her body until her face touched the cold stone exterior of the lofty structure. Risking half her face away from the hidden positions, she saw a gathering at the center of the interior open ground. The figures were short and rail-thin, their arms and legs twitching awkwardly as they moved. The pale light only gave a glimpse of the children, which Lauren knew them to be.

She counted half a dozen in all; none older than ten or eleven, she guessed. Their malady was not evident, but a determined stare showed each of them was marked with one eye milky white, void of human quality. The vision jogged her memory, and she thought of the dreadful ceremony on the highest platform of the pyramid. The boy who stood before her on the dais was digesting in the festering gullet of the wicked god they worshiped. Their pale skin stood out among the dark people and marked them as outsiders.

"It's not their children," she whispered. "Stolen." The word stung her, and for a brief moment, she forgot Professor Markinson was there.

"Children of the mark," he said as he leaned out beyond her shoulder. "I have read about bizarre rituals meant to produce such things."

"Things?" Lauren protested sharply. "They're children."

"They're made to watch—" he stumbled over his words "—certain rituals. Furthermore, the result allows them to see."

Lauren froze. She peered back at him. "See what?" she asked hesitantly.

The professor watched the abomination. "Into the abyss." He looked at her. "To see into the netherworld."

Lauren did not know what he was talking about, but there was enough loathing in his voice to drive the terror home. She kept her eyes on the children. A collar bound each of them at the neck with a rope holding them to a stake dug into the ground.

"They're not like the boy I ran into in the pyramid," she said.

"You were in the pyramid?" he asked, amazed.

Lauren cringed as his voice rose. She scanned the gatherings at the far side of the buildings and the fissure in the cavern wall.

"Sorry," he added, barely at a whisper.

"It's not important," she said. "The boy I saw was in control of himself."

Professor Markinson's feet shifted on the rock as he repositioned himself next to her. "From what I can remember, few of the subjects survive the ritual," he explained. "I suppose I mistook the information to say the children died."

"Perhaps they become something much worse," she finished for him.

Lauren could not take her eyes off them. They appeared to be oblivious of one another. Their mindless twitching left them lashing out at the dark air in the direction of the closest member of the tribe. There was no sense of urgency here, not from the cursed children nor the natives busy at their task.

"We're wasting our time," the professor declared. Lauren heard the grinding of his teeth between his words. "We can't save them. Ahmed was wrong."

Lauren stepped away from the opening and turned to face him. She pulled the gun from her pocket and held it up where he could see it.

"I followed you, and look where it got me," she said. "This is what you wanted, right? This is what you were looking for the entire time." She motioned at the mighty pyramid and then made sure the safety was off. "Be careful what you wish for."

"What are you doing?"

Lauren heard him, but she was finished caring about his concerns. She had always taken pride in doing things her way and, more importantly, being strong enough to act independently. She was well aware that she was probably going to die. Lauren wanted to make one final attempt to save herself without the fear of Morgainok crushing her will.

"Stay close to me," she said, as the last offer of assistance to a man who did not deserve it. "We'll only get one shot at this."

Lauren had a plan. The validity of that plan was questionable even after she stepped out into the open. The free-flowing strategy came to her when she realized the children of the mark were trying to get their hands on their captives. It was not until she aimed that a troubling thought crossed through her mind.

I wonder how many rounds I have left.

Lauren could not account for the surge of courage pushing through her veins. A moment of clearness blocked out the dark faces turning toward her. The sudden peace allowed her to ignore the figure rushing at her from the base of the cavern wall. She walked toward the collared children and stopped outside their arms' reach.

A flash of memories came in an instant. Her grandfather taught her to shoot. She thought warmly of the kindness in his eyes as she took a breath, blew it halfway out, and then held it. It was how he taught her, and now she would use it to save herself.

The trigger slid back in a calm, even pull. Lauren barely heard the gun go off over the rising chorus of vile shrieks. The flash of light told her all she needed to know. The shot found its mark, splintering the wooden spike in the ground.

The sudden shift in the air was so bewildering that Lauren felt for a moment that she was in some terrible trance. The all-engulfing dread radically shifted as the children realized they were free. The unholy creations struck with animalistic reflexes, lashing out at anyone within their reach. The tribespeople now ran from the site in a panic.

Chaos filled the open space between the structures and the cavern wall. The marked children lurched at the fleeing crowd, some latching on to escaping figures and instantly yanking them to the ground. Bloodcurdling screams marked the beginning of the slaughter. It took Lauren a horrified second to catch up with the scene.

She ran straight ahead, keeping her eyes on the fissure in the cavern wall. The line of tribespeople scattered, some attempting to push their way forward but most dropping their baskets and running. Lauren did not look back for Professor Markinson; the gnawing fright in her gut would not allow her to take her eyes off her goal. There was nothing to guarantee the fissure or the ledge high above offered any hope of safety, but her mind needed something to hold onto.

The mass spread around her. A few of them slammed into Lauren with no more concern for her than they had for the baskets they left behind. The terror of the children was complete, and the justification quickly became evident. One of the little girls crossed in front of Lauren, racing on all fours. She leaped up in a single bound and hit one of the bolting men head-on.

The impact drove the man back several feet before the pair slapped the ground. The girl dug her fingers into his eyes the moment his head smacked the solid rock. He screamed as blood spurted up between her hands. She pitched her head back, baying up into the darkness overhead until the man stopped twitching.

Lauren hurdled the man's legs as the girl plucked her fingers from his eye socket and reached for her. A firm hand slapped Lauren's shin, pulling her leg out from under her, and the impact sent her sprawling forward. She hit the ground on her stomach. The force knocked the wind out of her and sent the gun sliding ahead. Terror kept Lauren going, scrambling to her feet.

She did not look back, not even when the fiendish howl closed in. Lauren took her eyes off the fissure in the wall long enough to find the gun. She leaned over to swipe it off the ground when the girl crashed into her from behind. They tumbled over one another, ending with Lauren sitting on the wild girl's chest.

Lauren arched her back as fingernails ripped through her shirt and tore at her skin. Heat swelled from the cuts as blood broke the surface. Lauren jumped up and did not recognize she had recovered the gun until she was in a full sprint. The professor was ahead of her now with little concern for anyone or anything he left behind.

Several long strides fully exposed the fissure in the cavern wall. Carved steps lined the narrow gap, ascending the smooth rocky face. Silhouetted figures climbed frantically up the stairs, pushing and shoving one another as they went racing away from one of the marked children. Professor Markinson reached the fissure and started up the stairs two at a time.

Lauren was a stride away from the first step before she looked back. The marked girl vaulted toward her on all fours, mouth open, teeth exposed, and the single milky eye bulging in the socket. Lauren slammed herself to one side of the opening, and the wild girl swept past her in midair. The girl caught Professor Markinson at the knees, and his entire body snapped backward and tumbled down head over foot. He came to a rest on his backside, sitting directly in front of Lauren. The professor sat frozen, his face filled with the fright of the marked girl spinning around and looking down at him. Lauren stepped in front of him and raised the gun, still uncertain if she had another round to use.

"Get away from me," Lauren roared.

The girl hissed and slashed at the air between them but did not come any closer. The standoff lasted another hiss before the girl titled her head like a dog and then started up the stairs without warning. Lauren waited until she disappeared around a bend before lowering the gun. Professor Markinson pushed past her and started his climb without so much as a word. Lauren let out a growl of her own before taking the first step, her aggravation spitting out between clenched teeth.

"You're welcome."

15

Lauren quickly caught up with Professor Markinson and thought to give him a shove as she vaulted past him. He sucked in mouthfuls of air as if each one might be his last. The angle of the climb rose sharply, and a glance ahead revealed an awaiting hand-over-hand ascent. The marked child was already dangling from the stone-carved rungs, swiftly climbing higher and higher.

Figures dotted the ledge along the cavern wall, most of them running away from a frenzied gathering near the lip of the stairs. The group fractured, sending two bodies over the side. Lauren watched them fall, one screaming as he did, the other lifeless before he ever smashed into the cavern floor. The marked child cleared the climb before Lauren, and the professor reached the first rung. The stairs continued beyond the top of the carved ladder, rising at a severe incline all the way to the top.

Lauren placed the gun in her pocket and grabbed onto the first rung with both hands. The deep scratches in her back throbbed as her skin stretched. She shimmied her way up, nearly losing her strength before she could get a good foothold to keep herself going. A startled shout brought her to a stop.

"It's coming."

Lauren looked down at the top of Professor Markinson's head. He was gawking the way they came; his finger extended toward something rushing up after them. The pale light revealed the *something* was actually two *someones*. The open ground between the semicircle of structures and the cavern wall was bare, with only the faint sound of the terrible drums echoing off the rock. The last of the children of the mark had taken to the stairway and were fast approaching the stragglers.

"Help me," the professor pleaded as his frantic eyes looked up at Lauren. "Grab my hand." He jumped straight up and latched onto the bottom rung, his mouth still moving. "Don't leave me here."

Lauren reached without thinking and grabbed the professor by the wrist. He felt like dead weight in her hand. The load yanked her away from the ladder, leaving her clinging on by her fingertips. She tried not to look at the heinous figures closing in.

"Pull me—"

"I can't."

The first marked boy pulled out of the shadows, and his contorted face flashed a violent sneer as he let out a shriek. Lauren heaved until the tips of her fingers gave. She had to force herself to let go of the professor. The old man yelled a nasty curse before latching onto Lauren's leg.

The sudden clench pulled her entire body away from the wall. Had she not pressed down with her feet, she would have slipped right off the ladder. Lauren responded from instinct, kicking at Professor Markinson before he pulled her down to their doom. Her boot made solid contact with his face, but the man would not let go. The professor reached up and seized her belt with one hand and a rung in the stone-carved ladder with the other.

She started climbing the second the professor released her belt. Lauren neither confirmed he was climbing nor looked back to see if the wild children had caught up with him. She was up to the level ground in moments and started for the next set of stairs. Lauren took two or three steps at a time as her mind felt an abrupt sensation of being rounded up for the slaughter.

She knew there were at least two of the children somewhere above and another group closing in behind. The countless tribespeople up on the ledge would no doubt turn their attention to her once the children were subdued or killed. Rising awareness of the vast blackness hovering over Morgainok closed in around her. The overwhelming malevolence of the elder thing hidden by the darkness rained down on the insignificant woman fighting for her life.

Pain consumed her, from countless cuts and scratches to the burning strain on her muscles. None of it would ultimately compare to the unmeasurable damage to her mind. She had glimpsed the netherworld and beheld elder things that should not or could not walk the earth. The totality of her journey into the abyss might break her grip on sanity if she dared to consider it. The insurmountable terror was the only thing keeping her in the moment.

The narrow path turned sharply from one direction to the next, always ascending higher. The professor's wheezing breaths were close, followed by the atrocious shrieks of the marked children and the ever-present pounding drums. Lauren pushed herself, even when her legs begged her to stop. Her lungs were on fire in her chest as she huffed for every breath.

Lauren did not slow down until the elusive ledge was a few steps away. She caught sight of a series of bodies strewn out along the leveled path. A quick glimpse revealed at least one of the dead as a marked girl and the others tribesmen. The girl was marred with punctures along the chest, blood pooling around her lifeless body. The tribesmen were in a ravaged state, missing portions of skin along the face and neck.

The heinous scene was lost after a few steps, carefully avoiding the blood and human debris. Lauren slowed to a crawl. The pale glow in the rock had little power here on the cliff, and the darkness hanging over the city shrouded the way ahead. She could hardly see more than moving shadows a few long strides ahead of her.

"What are you doing?" Professor Markinson asked as he overtook her with his back pressed up against the cavern wall. He looked between the lip of the ledge and the top of the stone steps behind them. "We have to keep moving."

Lauren took one glance out at the magnificent drop over the side of the ledge and snapped her head back. She pulled the gun from her pocket and clasped the grip tightly. The feel of the metal in the palm of her hand produced a swell of courage. The professor stopped and watched her, unwilling to go any farther without her by his side.

Lauren took a moment of clarity to check the weapon and found four bullets remaining. A slap of her palm and tug on the slide ensured she had a round in the chamber. She spun around in time to catch the first of the marked boys rise up to the ledge. Lauren pulled the trigger the instant she saw the center of his milky eye. The round caught him above the cheek and sent his head snapping back. His body fell instantly limp, crumbling on the top step in a pile of lifeless matter.

"Three," she said, keeping a close count of the remaining rounds. "Let's go."

She nudged her chin forward, and the professor moved without hesitation. He stayed beside her as the two moved forward, both leaning away from the edge of the cliff. Lauren tried to keep one eye on the way behind them and the other on the way ahead. She knew at least one of the marked children remained on the stairs, and it would only be a matter of time before they caught up with the fray in front. The time was far shorter than she imagined.

A wall of arms and legs came out of the shadows: a group of dark-skinned tribesmen pressing against one another in a mad frenzy. Lauren counted three before they were on to her, each of them yowling in a terrible craze. The force of the crowd bowled her down before she ever thought to fire her weapon. Two of the men trampled across her chest and continued on their way, but the third man stumbled before plummeting over the side of the cliff.

Lauren sat up, dazed from the impact, and the dark world spun out of control around her. She swayed as she tried to stand. One hand against the cavern wall kept her up, but the way ahead drifted in and out of view. She recognized Professor Markinson running away from her and spotted the gun in his hand a second before the shadows swallowed him.

"You ass," she roared as her senses abruptly returned. "You are the absolute worst."

She took a shaky step and then another. Lauren moved forward with a noticeable slant to her right. She nearly dropped one foot off the edge of the cliff before leaping sideways. The acrobatic move would have made her snicker had it not been terrifying.

"Professor Markinson."

She kept herself going, barreling down the narrow ledge with mad abandonment. Lauren was determined to catch up with the professor. Something about his willingness to desert her so quickly burned deep down in her belly. She got her wish quicker than she thought she would.

The mighty cavern wall bent at a sharp slant, and the pathway hugged the turn. Lauren was running as fast as her legs would carry her. The view opened up ahead, but she was moving too quickly to stop before it was too late. The sound of a fight exploded as the ledge widened.

Professor Markinson's fair skin stood out among the ebony bodies. Several of the natives formed an arc at the pathway's widest point. The professor stood on the far side of the gathering, his back to Lauren. Several of the men jabbed spears and swung knives at the cavern wall. It took Lauren a few steps to realize that the professor was not the target of their wrath.

A young girl leaned back against the cavern wall, hunched over, slashing her hands at the violent crowd. She growled at the on-lookers, biting at the air as they screamed at her. Blood ran down her exposed chest from several wounds. A gash in her leg said she would not survive much longer.

Lauren never stopped moving. She figured that if she were going to survive, she would have to get around the natives. The turn of the pathway placed the pale glowing view of Morgainok behind her. Shadows grew darker ahead, deepening to a pitch-black beyond the gathering. Lauren focused on the professor and found his terrified eyes peering back at her.

She saw the gun in his hands as he managed to back away from the group on the far side of the crowd. A pair of the tribesmen turned away from the marked child and followed him. Lauren was a step away before any of them noticed. She caught a glimpse of a spear-head catching the young girl in the throat. The marked child shuddered as she spit blood up into the air.

The sound of a gunshot refocused Lauren's attention. One tribesman lay on the ground at the professor's feet, but the other was undeterred. A monstrous roar arose from the gathering behind her as their motivation shifted from the dying girl to the fleeing sacrifices. A tribesman jabbed at her with the tail end of his spear and caught Lauren off guard. The weapon clipped her on the hip with teeth-rattling force.

The impact sent Lauren lurching forward in an uncoordinated roll. She landed on her back and slid to a stop an inch from going over the edge of the cliff. The gun went off again before she caught her bearings. Lauren sat up as her side erupted. She did not need to see the mob of natives to know they were coming. The last thing she expected was to find Professor Markinson aiming the gun at her head.

"Stay down," he yelled, his eyes on the ferocious group behind her. "Stay down," he repeated before turning to run.

"The hell with that," she grunted the instant he spun around.

Lauren's knee buckled as she tested her weight. She had to drive her good leg down as if she was performing a squat press to get her body to remain erect. The pain intensified as she took a step, but she ground her teeth and kept going. The pitch-black darkness lay ahead, and it nearly swallowed the professor when his body stiffened. Lauren did not see the spear dug deep into his back until another throw shot by, missing her head by a hair.

Professor Markinson fell first to his knees and then dropped face down. The spear sprang up like a flag planted in his back. The last bit of Morgainok's light glinted off the gun in his hand. Lauren leaned over him and wrenched the weapon free. She took a single step before he latched onto her ankle.

"Help me," he croaked in a raspy voice.

Lauren responded by stomping on his wrist. The professor heaved and then howled. His grip released, and Lauren was free. She plunged into the darkness with the gun clenched in one hand and the other sliding along the cavern wall.

The black veil was all-encompassing. Lauren could not see her hand in front of her face. She refused to slow down, using the sounds of the trailing pack as a motivator. An overwhelming sense of dread pressed in on her like a vice. She was certain she would either fall off the cliff and plummet to her death or end up with a wide array of spears and blades dug deep into her back.

The chaotic sounds intensified all at once, and the thought occurred to her that she had slipped into a side passage. She did not dare test her theory or reach out for the other side of the pathway and see if another cavern wall awaited her. The drumming was loud, so much so, she imagined more of the tribe had climbed up onto the ledge after her and had joined the hunt.

Madness brewed deep within Lauren's mind. The darkness had a way of heightening fear, and her horrors were nearby. Her pace slowed to a slither as the terror overwhelmed her. Reaching out into the darkness, her hand touched something soft, and she recoiled. The recognition struck as she reached out again. Lauren ran her fingers over a solid piece of wood sectioned between two segments of rope.

She lifted her leg and found her footing. The rope ladder swayed as Lauren started her climb. She had no idea where the ladder led, but the mere fact that it was ascending out of the godforsaken city was enough. The trailing echoes reached a fever pitch as they crashed into the rock below her. The ladder swayed violently and then continued with a constant shudder riding up the ropes.

Lauren climbed hand over hand, foot over foot until every fiber of her body screamed at her to stop. The wound on her hip throbbed until she thought her leg might disconnect itself from the rest of her slender frame. She shouted into the darkness as the madness fought for control, but she never stopped climbing. Nefarious shouts rose up at her, and she expected some vile thing to grab her at any moment.

A glimmer of hope flickered through the dark from a pinpoint of light. The soft glow was faint and distant, but it was there in the center of the vast nothingness overhead. Lauren kept her eyes on it, and the widening expanse inspired her to climb faster, ignoring the agonizing torment pumping through her limbs. The distance felt impossibly far until a glimpse of the crescent moon confirmed the hope of freedom.

Fresh air filled Lauren's lungs as she reached out through an opening and pulled herself up. Moonlight revealed the hole in the ground and a circle of man-sized stones. Soaring trees on all sides blocked out the surrounding landscape. Lauren thought to run, but the heinous sounds rising from the black pit held her still.

She quickly gathered the largest rocks she could carry, and one by one, she dropped them into the hole and waited. A piercing scream quickly rewarded her notion. Several shrieks followed the first, and Lauren was satisfied that she had bought herself some time. She rushed into the trees and discovered the sparse grove let out onto a wide basin. The endless view offered no hints about its location or its approximation to where the disastrous adventure began. She ran out into the open expanse, dragging one leg with increasing difficulty. A quick pat confirmed she still possessed the gun and a mental note told her the last round would not last long.

She staggered for miles, stopping to look back every couple of strides. The exhausting effort finally wore into her bones. Lauren thought she would have to walk into oblivion until the coarse grass beneath her feet gave way to a wide stretch of dirt running off to the east and west. She stopped dead center and let the discovery sink in.

"A road."

Confirmation soon followed in the form of piercing lights. Sparkling diamonds in the dark hovered off the ground, turning directly toward her in the distance. Lauren never moved, not even when the roaring sound of the diesel engine bore down on her. The tires flung dirt in the air as the brakes locked. The truck came to a stop, hardly a foot in front of her.

The man behind the wheel waved his arms, offering a string of directions in his native tongue. Lauren stumbled around the side of the truck and headed for the bed of the cattle car. Several figures sat against metal slatted sides, none of them offering her a hint of assistance. No one spoke as she struggled to climb the ladder over the rear gate. She fell onto the hard flat bottom, clinging to consciousness as her rescuing chariot roared to life and continued on its way.

◆

Lauren sat crumpled against the rear railing of the cattle car, her knees up close to her face. The makeshift people mover constantly rattled as if the entire thing might fall apart at any moment. The pain in her hip pulsed with her heartbeat, riding up her spine and then down the side of her leg. Her wild eyes were on the figures lining the benches.

They were men, nearly two dozen by quick count, most of them shirtless. Their dark hair and darker skin placed them as commoners in the area, who made their lives outside the major cities. The men faced forward, not one bothering to spare a glance at Lauren. She was grateful to be ignored.

Lauren took her eyes off the view and ducked her head between her knees. She breathed in until it hurt and tried to blow out the pain as she exhaled. She closed her eyes, but the visions of what she had seen flashed through her mind. Her eyes sprang open as a gasp escaped her mouth. The sight of the elder thing burned into her soul, and she feared she would never be able to close her eyes again.

The horror sped up her heart, and the pounding filled her ears. She could not distinguish the beat from the abhorrent thumping of the drums of Morgainok. She shook her head in an attempt to make it all go away, but another sound replaced it. The word was low, barely above a whisper, but growing. Lauren focused on the sound, and she knew the name at once.

NasNoroth

Her head snapped up, and she peered in wide-eyed terror at a man at the front of the flatbed. He stood and faced her. His eyes stared into her soul. He mouthed the name again, and another man quickly echoed it.

"NasNoroth."

One by one, they stood, each man turning to face her as they rose.

"NasNoroth."

They repeated the name of the vile thing over and again.

"NasNoroth."

Every man was standing when the truck began its turn. Lauren could not breathe. She could not bring herself to scream. The sheer horror of the sight before her stole the breath from her lungs. The truck headed back in the opposite direction before the men on the flatbed started toward her.

"NasNoroth."

Lauren found her voice as she forced herself to stand. "Get the hell away from me."

She slid her hand over the top of the railing as the closest man reached out for her.

"NasNoroth."

Lauren drew her gun and fired.

THE END

THE GRIEF THAT LINGERS

Rise of the Elder

Book II

By

Michael W. Garza

1

Benjamin Hack was a simple man who lived his life sullen and alone. His tall, gangly features promised him reclusiveness, and Benjamin would have it no other way. He shied from social contact and had little temperament for small talk. The nature of his personality was to draw away into the recesses of society and leave others to their own devices.

The old brick home at 124 Hamilton Street was similar to its owner. The poorly maintained exterior hid a cold and dreary interior. The people of New Haven, Connecticut, knew nothing about the home, and like its owner, the old brick residence liked it that way.

The whole of his life could be measured in a few simple failures, most of which he blamed on his parents in one fashion or another.

At twenty-seven, he was alone and nearly penniless. Everything he had once belonged to his father. The elder Hack and his fateful bride perished some nineteen months prior in a sailing accident, leaving Benjamin a sizable inheritance.

Benjamin managed to squander his newfound wealth with considerable flair, visiting countless high prized bars and clubs located in the seedier parts of New Haven, Connecticut. Women, wine, and feasts produced a string of hanger-on's, none of which would return his calls. The product of his final bank withdrawal stood in a row on the kitchen counter, most of the bottles empty from a weekend binge Benjamin was still fighting to overcome. The money was gone.

He sat up in bed, throwing his legs off the edge. His bare feet touched the cold wooden floorboards sending a chill up his back. Benjamin looked down at himself in disgust. His potbelly was a revolting reminder of the needless wasting of his funds.

It took him considerable energy to convince himself to stand up. The motion caused the room to swirl as the missing contents of the bottle by his bed played havoc on his head. Benjamin stumbled forward and caught himself on the windowsill. He unlocked the bolt and slid up the windowpane in search of fresh air.

The perfectly timed sounds of New Haven harbor greeted him. The afternoon arrival of fishing boats mixed with dockhand calls and conversations. The smell of fresh fish was pungent. Benjamin hated fish, and the aroma made him even more nauseated.

He slumped backward and hit the floor on his backside. Benjamin sat on the floor, gathering himself long enough to let his stomach finish its churn. He descended to the first floor and took in the hovel in one sweeping glance. Piles of clothes and assorted food containers lined the front hall in no discernable order.

Benjamin crossed into the front room and slumped down on the chair facing the wide bay window overlooking Hamilton Street. He down the remainder of a cup sitting on the crowded table beside the chair and eyed the growing stack of bills staring back at him. None of the envelopes was open, but he did not need to read them to know their intent. The letters began to arrive several months prior, and he guessed the latest editions contained words such as *Final Notice* and *Foreclosure*. Benjamin had not worked in several years. He realized that if he planned to eat in the very near future, he had better do something about it soon.

He ate a bit of cold bread and washed it down with another cup of yesterday's brew. He avoided one of the taller stacks of books randomly placed about the house and headed back to his chair. His descent into the well-worn cushions shoved the side table, and the result sent the stack of envelopes tumbling to the ground. He cursed if for nothing else to hear something break the veil of silence cloaking the house.

Benjamin was determined to spend the day drowning his sorrows in the bottom of one of the reaming bottles of overpriced Scotch. He took a firm grip on his glass and decided to get to it when something caught his eye on the floor. The countless envelopes covered the floor at his feet, most of them adorned with the familiar markings of a local provider of some sort—a hand-scrawled name, which stood out from everything else.

Edward Hack had been a renowned psychologist at Ashland Asylum. His stature in New Haven provided a comfortable life for Benjamin and his mother; however, the elder Hack's hidden interests had a profound impact on his son. Edward had been a Medical officer in the army and developed a macabre interest in life and death. He carried his interest into his civilian life, spending his time acquiring knowledge of a perverted nature. A good portion of the books and aged tomes strewed about the home were of archaic knowledge.

Benjamin hesitantly leaned forward as if the thing might bite him. The closer he came, the more the writing became clear. It was addressed to his father with no return address. Benjamin pushed the bills out of the way and studied the letter in question, ask closely as he could without touching it. The stand was marked clearly in red with the date. Benjamin did the calculation in his head and determined the letter had to have been mailed out only days before his parents died.

He snatched the dispatch up with considerable force then brought it close to his chest as he leaned back. He hunched over the letter, running his eyes along the front bay window. The traffic on Hamilton Street continued on its way, unconcerned with the pathetic goings-on inside the house at 124. The room darkened before his eyes as a billow of clouds rolled in from the east.

Benjamin turned the envelope over and was struck by the blood-red seal marking the fold. Timidly, he slid his finger over the circular image and found a connection as a flash of memory caught his mind. The open eye pierced by a single thorn gazed back at him as if watching his every move. Benjamin quickly slid his finger under the flat and snapped the seal. He removed a single page of stationery, unfolded the sheet, and read.

Undoubtedly, the Elders will come for you. The calling is upon us, and those faithful to NasNoroth have chosen. You alone should not possess the treasure, and your faithful brother seeks to share in your rebirth. Come to me with your tremendous gift, or I shall reveal to Ashland what you have taken.

J.R.H

Sudden sobriety washed over Benjamin as the full content of the message came to him. There was a true terror in-between the words that struck him, which he could not place. He found it difficult to breathe, and the darkness rolling into his home suddenly enclosed around him. He peered at the corners of the space with a sudden interest to absorb the rest of the room.

Benjamin's hands shook as he tried to refold the letter. He managed to place it back in the envelope and then tossed the thing on the table. It lay there leering at him like a snake, its edges shifting in an unseen wind like a rattler. He pushed himself up off the chair and rushed into the kitchen, pushing over the empty bottles on the counter until he found the one he wanted.

The bottle of Scotch trembled as Benjamin tried to pour another drink. He found the task too difficult and pulled straight from the top. His nerves were beyond him, and the words of the letter clung to the recesses of his mind. NasNoroth, the Elders, Ashland, he had heard these before. The books strewn about the house contained volumes dedicated to such things.

Benjamin had inherited an interest in ghastly things from his father. His eyes had seen foul incantations written in languages few could read. He knew the evils of NasNoroth and read of the existence of the Cult of the Elder, although he did not believe in them. His father had been a true believer in the so-called greater gods.

Benjamin eyed the letter from across the front room as he drank. There was no want in him to pick it up, but a single word stuck to him, *treasure*. Rumors about the Hack family ran deep and wide, and Benjamin knew them all. At that moment, one such rumor, in particular, came back to him.

The family line ran deep through the founders of New Haven, although they were never among the noteworthy types. Grave robbers, devil worshipers, and thieves were designations earned throughout the family's history. The accounts of Edward Hack's fortune were a closely guarded secret, one Benjamin knew very little about. He did, however, remember a conversation with his father's brother nearly a decade ago.

The memory came to Benjamin in fleeting details. There was something about a stolen treasure and an accusation by the believers of the Cult of the Elder. Benjamin slumped down in the chair, taking a long drink from his bottle, his thoughts drifting to the possibility of truth among the salacious rumors.

A haze washed across his concerns as the alcohol began to do its work. The fear within Benjamin remained, but his newfound strength encouraged him to continue. He was desperate, and any hope, no matter how dark or wound in the clutches of the Cult of the Elder, was something he could ignore. A deep breath and another long drink allowed him to turn his attention back to the letter.

The envelope lay on the table, its broken seal staring back at him. Benjamin stared at it, searching through his clouding memory for a hint at where he had seen it before. The answer came in one quick jolt. The recognition brought him up to his feet, spilling the remainder of his Scotch on the hardwood floor.

Benjamin rushed into the hallway, kicking the bottle of Scotch across the floor as he went. He headed directly for the broad black door in the hall beneath the stairs. The basement was not somewhere he liked to spend his time. The endless creates and boxes marked the entire contents of his father's precious belongings, soothing he had no interest in until that particular moment. Benjamin used the dark space as a hiding place in his youth, daring himself to remain there until his father would come search for him. A particular belt whipping ended the childish game on his ninth birthday, leaving marks that remained to this very day.

It took considerable effort to pull the door open. Benjamin stood at the top of the stairs staring down at the complete blackness. He knew the single source of light dangled from a cord in the center of the basement. He would have to work his way through the dark to reach it.

Each step creaked beneath his weight, signaling his descent. Benjamin stopped once his feet tapped the concrete floor. A chill struck him in the chest as he froze, trying desperately to see through the darkness. For a moment, he was that nine-year-old boy again, terrified of the dark, and more so his father. He had to force himself to move, stretching his hands out in front of him. The black closed around him and his mind filled with all of the terrible depictions he glimpsed in his father's fiendish tomes.

Flashes of the gargantuan NasNoroth floated overhead as a shadow of the vile Suleak stalked toward him. His heart thundered in his chest until it pounded in his ears. Benjamin screamed as something slid across his face. He turned to run only to realize the attacker was the pull string he was searching for. Benjamin caught hold of the chain and pulled.

The feeble bulb sent lines of pale light over a sea of stacked good. Most of the contents were draped with dust-covered sheets, hiding their secrets underneath. Benjamin's eyes went to the lone trunk lying in open view. The rich leather exterior was lined with metal edging, and its formidable lock glared up at him, daring him to attempt entry.

Benjamin ignored the lock for now. He knew at once that his memory had served him well. His eyes found the mark he was searching for, carved into the trunk's ornate surface. His hands trembled against his leg as he took in the view of an open eye pierced by a single thorn gazing back at him.

ABOUT THE AUTHOR

Michael W. Garza often finds himself wondering where his inspiration will come from next and in what form his imagination will bring it to life. The outcomes regularly surprise him, and it is always his ambition to amaze those curious enough to follow him and take in those results. He hopes everyone will find something that frightens, surprises, or astonishes them.